—

Jill Wolfson

WHAT
I CALL
LIFE

Henry Holt and Company
New York

CH

Henry Holt and Company, LLC
Publishers since 1866
175 Fifth Avenue
New York, New York 10010
www.henryholtchildrensbooks.com

Henry Holt® is a registered trademark of Henry Holt and Company, LLC.
Copyright © 2005 by Jill Wolfson

Library of Congress Cataloging-in-Publication Data
Wolfson, Jill.
What I call life / Jill Wolfson.—1st ed.
p.   cm.
Summary: Placed in a group foster home, eleven-year-old Cal Lavender learns how to
cope with life from the four other girls who live there and from their storytelling
guardian, the Knitting Lady.
ISBN-13: 978-0-8050-7669-1
ISBN-10: 0-8050-7669-7
[1. Foster home care—Fiction.   2. Self-perception—Fiction.   3. Storytelling—
Fiction.   4. Conduct of life—Fiction.   5. Knitting—Fiction.]   I. Title.
PZ7.W8332Wh 2005   [Fic]—dc22   2004060742

First Edition—2005
Printed in the United States of America on acid-free paper. ∞

1   3   5   7   9   10   8   6   4   2

To Alex and Gwen—
my inspiration for everything,
even sunflower seeds

CHAPTER 1

Everyone is always living her story.

When I first heard this, I thought: *What kind of nutty philosophy is that? Who would buy it? Everyone? Always?*

All I had to do was look at my own personal situation to see how wrongheaded this kind of thinking happened to be. I looked around at where I was living at the time and with whom I was living and shook my head. *No, sir. This isn't MY story. This is nothing like MY life.*

My life—what I call life—had been running its usual course up until recently. Until everything came to a complete and total halt. That was the day my mother happened to have one of her episodes in full public view at the library (more on that later). I, for a fact, knew that things weren't as bad as they might look. Anyone who knew my mother knew that she'd snap out of it eventually. She always did.

But certain people in the library didn't look too kindly on some of the things she was doing during her episode. So these certain people called the police, and, while one of the officers whisked my mother one way, another whisked me outside and loaded me into the back seat of his patrol car.

That had been my first time ever in a police car, and, while I suppose that most eleven-year-old girls would have thrown a full-blown emotional conniption, I didn't put up a fuss, no fuss at all.

Which brings me back to the subject of life stories. If I was going to tell mine, that's one of the first things I would put in about myself: *Cal Lavender is known far and wide for never fussing.*

No crying. No whining. No complaining. No fuss. Not even when she has to sit in a police car, breathing in the smell of sweat, stale cigarettes, and worn, cracked leather. Whew! I'll tell you one thing. If that vehicle is any indication of what the rest of the police cars in our city are like, they could definitely use a good airing out. But even though I have the ability to clean up far worse messes, I wasn't about to volunteer to do it. Let that officer and his criminal riders clean out their own car.

There was a sharp crackle of static from the police radio, and that's when I decided that I would fold up and die right then and there if the policeman put on the siren. I cringed at the thought of being paraded through downtown in such an embarrassing manner, especially so soon after the previous embarrassing situation at the library. (Like I already said, more on that later.)

That's another thing you could put in any story about my life: *Cal Lavender hates it when nosy strangers think it is perfectly okay to stare at people in situations that they know nothing about.*

But thank goodness the siren didn't happen. There were only the usual traffic noises. I was perfectly anonymous, just the way I like to be. I pressed my nose against the window. I looked out at the streaks of stores and buses and people rushing by, but nobody could see in. For all anyone knew, the car contained a cold-blooded killer/arsonist/drug dealer on her way to the electric chair, instead of an eleven-year-old girl with a mother who unfortunately happens to have episodes every once in a while. Which, to my way of thinking, does not come anywhere near qualifying as a criminal offense.

Every so often, I caught the policeman sneaking peeks at me through the rearview mirror. When he saw me looking back, he snapped his eyes away. But then he would look again when he thought I wasn't looking. Then I would snap *my* eyes away. We went back and forth like that for a while, until we stopped at a red light. This time, he didn't drop his eyes. "No problems back there—right, young lady?"

His eyes held on to mine, which made me feel kind of funny in the stomach, even though I'm sure I didn't show it. I have spent many hours in front of a mirror, imagining embarrassing situations even worse than this one and making sure that, whatever jumpy feeling was going on inside of me, I, Cal Lavender, would have the same fixed expression on my face. I call it My Face for Unbearably Unpleasant and Embarrassing Situations. It looks like this: Eyes like two black checkers. Mouth, a thin line with only the slightest curve at the corners. I'm naturally olive-skinned and thin, with one long eyebrow instead of the two short ones that ordinary people have. This gives me the ability to scowl without even trying. My mother, who has the same line across her forehead, says it's an awning over our eyes, protection against whatever life throws at us.

That's the face I showed the policeman, which made him cough nervously and then say, "Hey, would you like one of these breath-mint things? Sure, all kids like breath mints." A tin of Altoids landed next to me. I didn't touch it. "Not *all* kids think that their breath needs help," I said.

"No offense intended," he said back.

I forgave him. I had seen the name on his tag—Officer Quiggly—and immediately renamed him in my mind. Officer Quiggly Wiggly. That's another thing I inherited from my mother. She has a way of finding the perfect name for everyone, me included. (More on that later, too.)

Then there was more crackling from the radio. "Yeah, that's where we're headed," Quiggly Wiggly said into the receiver. The light changed to green, and the car moved forward.

Now, your average eleven-year-old would probably have been scared out of her wits, not knowing where she was headed, where the ride was taking her, not knowing what waited ahead.

But not me. Not Cal Lavender. I wasn't scared at all. My knees were aligned, my thighs pressing together and perfectly matched. My hands were folded on my lap.

Why should I have been scared? After all, this wasn't my story. This was just a short, temporary detour from what I call life.

CHAPTER 2

When I first made the acquaintance of the Knitting Lady, the first thing she said to me was not *Everyone is always living her story.* That came later when she was telling us a fascinating tale that took us from coast to coast and covered about one hundred years of human history.

I have to say she turned out to be an excellent story-teller, even though I had my doubts when I first met her. There was the fact that she stuttered, not all the time, but enough that— Now there I go, jumping ten steps ahead.

I haven't even explained yet about the Knitting Lady. Who is she? How did I wind up on her doorstep? How did I meet the other girls who became my friends—no, they became more than friends—despite the fact that they drove me absolutely crazy?

I need to take a giant step back, return myself to the police car, and explain how I, Cal Lavender, came to be living a life that wasn't my own.

So.

I was in the police car, and we traveled on the freeway for a while. So far, I was doing fine with all this. To my way of thinking, travel can be very educational. Officer Quiggly Wiggly took an exit, then went a few more blocks before turning onto a narrow street with a one-way arrow. "Hang in there, young lady," he said. "We're just about home."

Home? Whose home? Not my home. I looked out the window and asked myself: *If this is home, where are all the rooming houses? Where's the bus station? Where's the Sacred Heart Community Center, where an eleven-year-old girl and her mother can walk in and pick out any kind of outfit she wants and it doesn't cost them one red cent?*

No, this definitely wasn't home. Here, all the houses were exactly alike and painted the exact same shade of not-exactly-white. The flowers on the lawns were perky and perfectly spaced, like they were doing a line dance. When the policeman clicked off the motor, everything came to a stop that felt strange and permanent, like nothing would ever move again.

I would say that this feeling was caused by a case of the nerves—if Cal Lavender was the type of person to have a case of the nerves, which she definitely is not.

I must have opened the car door. I must have walked, because the next thing I knew, Officer Quiggly Wiggly and I were standing on the front step of the only house that was orange instead of not-exactly-white. And I do mean orange. What had the painter been thinking? Officer

Quiggly Wiggly knocked on the door, and from the other side I heard footfalls and the shouting, laughing voices of what sounded to be about a million girls.

Then the door opened and I was standing forehead to forehead, eye to eye, with a woman. Even though I'm eleven and she looked to be about 111, we were the same height. Her cheekbones sat high on her face in two peaks. Her nose came to a point. That was my first impression of the Knitting Lady, sort of a Munchkin with white-gray hair pulled back into a neat, tight bun.

Behind her, the million girls were jostling one another to get a better opportunity to stare and point at me. "Officer," the woman said.

"Yes, ma'am. I'm assuming you got the call about this one."

"We're all r-ready for her."

"She's a nice, quiet one. Didn't give me a moment's trouble."

I made sure that My Face for Unbearably Unpleasant and Embarrassing Situations was perfect. I spoke clearly and slowly like a microphone was being held in front of my face. If I do say so myself, Cal Lavender is known for having a mature manner of speaking. "I assure you that I am never any trouble to anyone."

"Of course, you're no trouble, d-dear." Then she squinted at the policeman's badge. "Thank you, Officer Wiggly."

"Quiggly," he corrected.

"Quiggly?" she asked.

"Yes. It's Officer Quiggly, ma'am. You said 'Officer Wiggly.'"

"Oh, did I? Well, aren't I the silly one? Thanks again, Officer Wiggly. No! Officer Quiggly, not Wiggly. I'm sure she will fit in just w-wonderfully."

By this point, all the million girls were busting a gut from the Quiggly-Wiggly confusion. The Knitting Lady didn't smile though. But there was something behind her eyes—the look of club soda that had been shaken hard— that told me she knew exactly what she was doing. That was very interesting to me because I had never met any grown-ups—except my mother, of course—who didn't mind acting not too bright every once in a while.

Poor Officer Quiggly Wiggly. His mustache trembled a little in confusion as he tried to figure out whether or not she was making fun of him. Then he patted me on the shoulder. I gave him a polite, no-fuss-from-me smile and watched him walk away. "Okay, young lady," he yelled from the police car. "You're in good hands now."

Behind me, the woman laughed. She had a high, tinkling laugh, like it was bouncing off broken glass. "Hmmmm, good hands?" she asked. "Do these look like good hands to you?"

When I turned, she held her gnarled hands up to my face, all the fingers stretched out like she was teaching the number ten to a little kid. "I'd say these look more like old m-man hands, wouldn't you? I've seen people drop spare change into hands that look like these. But believe you me, they can still work the knitting needles."

"Knitting?" I asked.

"Knitting," she repeated. "Everyone here calls me the Knitting Lady. M-maybe I can teach you sometime. Think you might like to knit?"

"Perhaps that would be something I would enjoy," I said, but only to be polite.

"I knew it. I took one l-look at those nervous hands of yours and knew they were itching to try something new."

I had not even realized that my right hand was winding a strand of my hair around and around. Immediately, I dropped it, held both arms tight to my sides as though they were stitched there.

"Oh, don't be insulted," she said. "We all have our nervous habits. You should h-hear me stutter when my system gets overloaded. Besides, nervous hands are the best hands for knitting."

"My hands," I insisted, "are *not* nervous!" I closed my eyes to think better, and when I opened them again, I was ready to show that Cal Lavender was *never* nervous. "It's very kind of you to offer knitting instructions. But my mother will be coming for me soon. She doesn't do very well without me for long."

I couldn't help but notice how the Knitting Lady's forehead wrinkled with soft creases. Her mouth opened, then shut. Whatever it was that came to her mind, she forced it back in favor of just saying, "Ahhhh," accompanied by a dozen quick, light little pats on my shoulder.

I wondered, *What does "Ahhhh" mean?*

CHAPTER 3

"Girls," the Knitting Lady said, "the newest m-member of the household—Carolina Agnes London Indiana Florence Ohio Renee Naomi Ida Alabama Lavender."

I wanted to die. They didn't even try to do the polite thing and fight back the giggles.

We were in a large, sparsely furnished room that everyone referred to as Talk Central. It was the largest room in the house, probably some regular family's den before it got taken over by a bunch of girls with knitting needles in their hands and balls of yarn on their laps.

I was wrong about there being a million of them. It was more like four.

From what the Knitting Lady had explained so far, I had wound up in something called a group home. Which, from what I gathered, was a place that looked like a regular home from the outside, even if it was pumpkin-colored. But instead of one family living inside, this was where they put girls when their mothers had problems—like throwing an episode in a public place—and couldn't take care of them for the time being.

"That name's too long," one girl moaned. She was holding a pillow to her stomach. "I can't remember all that. I *caaaan't.*"

The girl sitting next to her started giggling and looking around the room with a spaced-out smile.

Another girl, this one so pale it looked like she had been through the wash too many times, bounded into the room like she owned it. Then she plopped on the floor and stared and stared like she also owned me.

This was my introduction to Whitney, one of my roommates-to-be. Didn't that girl ever comb her hair? She looked like she had a special brush just for *unbrushing* it. Plus, she had two silver front teeth instead of pearly white ones like the rest of us had. Her head was also way too big for her body.

That's when I noticed that Whitney wasn't the only one who looked like something had backed up and dinged her. The girl with the pillow was wearing a bright pink cast on her arm. And I don't know what the girl with the dopey smile had to smile about, since she had a right eye that was purple and swollen shut.

But strangest of all was the girl who had not yet said a word. Her problem was her hair. There's no way to put this politely. She had no hair. Well, it wasn't exactly *no* hair—she had something on her head, but it looked like a lawn mower had run wild on it. Her eyelashes and eyebrows were especially creepy. There *were* no eyelashes or eye-brows!

If I do say so myself, I'm very good at remembering names. Whitney was the one who never sat still. Monica was the big, doughy girl with the cast. Fern, thin with a face full of freckles, had the black eye. Amber was the one without hair, which made her face look like a lightbulb.

"Well, what's the story?" Whitney demanded.

The Knitting Lady clapped for silence. "Don't mind Whitney. She's a little, w-well, overly enthusiastic some-times. We'd all like to know the story of your name."

As I previously mentioned, I don't get nervous. I wasn't nervous then, definitely not. So probably I was hav-ing some kind of dust attack, because my voice came out in a squeak. "My mother . . . her name is Betty. I call her Betty." I hesitated. Just saying Betty's name out loud made me feel something like insects jumping around in my stomach. But for some reason, I wanted to keep saying her name as much as I could. So I did.

"Betty, you see, Betty named me for all the people she liked and all the places she passed through where good things happened to her. These are only a few of the places Betty has traveled. Betty is very well traveled. Betty says that traveling is very educational."

The whole time I was talking—which felt like about six hours—Fern kept giggling and the girl with no hair,

Amber, stared like she was storing up everything I was saying for an important test. On the other hand, Whitney was obviously the type who said every interesting and uninteresting thing that went through her mind. "That's a good one, all right. I like that story plenty. So what do we call you? You're gonna be my roommate, but I ain't gonna call you Alabama Alaska Ohio, or whatever you said."

The Knitting Lady had been quiet this whole time, looking very thoughtful, and then she said, "Oh!" Then "Oh!" again. "If you take the first letter from each name and state and line them up, it spells out *California.*"

Most people I have run into in my life are nowhere near that smart. I was impressed that she figured it out on her own. "Yes, California is where I was born. Betty says her luck had been running pretty good in California."

The Knitting Lady put down her needles. "So, you like it when people call you . . ."

"Cal," I said. "Everyone here can call me Cal."

CHAPTER 4

I was assigned to the largest bedroom on the second floor of the house. The walls were covered in pink paper with little embossed flowers. It was kind of pretty, except for the section where Whitney had scrawled her name—WHITNEY—all over it in printing that looked like it was done by a first grader. Three beds were lined up on one side. Mine was the middle one. It sat under a window that looked out onto a patio that had some dried-out crabgrass and a few spindly rosebushes.

Whitney threw herself on the bed to my right. Fern and Monica, who shared a room down the hall, stood between us. They were so close together, they could have been Siamese twins, except one was dark and little and the other was about twice her size.

"So Cal gal—" Whitney began.

"Cowgirl?" Fern interrupted. "Is she really a cowgirl?"

"Don't mind her," Whitney said to me. Then to Fern, "Fern, beat it, okay?"

I was shocked by such impoliteness, but Fern didn't seem to mind at all. She just shrugged, giggled, and headed out of the room. Monica followed close behind, complaining about being hungry.

"Are they always like that?" I wondered aloud.

"Like what?" Whitney asked.

"Like—" But that's all I got out because Whitney, who obviously lived to interrupt, interrupted me: "Forget about them. Who you really want to know about is me. I'm the girl who kicked heart disease's butt."

Then she reached for the edges of her shirt, and, just like that, pulled it up to her chin. A scar ran down from the hollow of her skinny neck and kept going until it disappeared over the edge of her belly button. Whitney noticed when I cringed, which seemed to please her no end. "Yep," she said. "Everyone gets grossed out."

After the unveiling of her scar, Whitney made a big production about showing me my dresser, which is where I was supposed to store all my personal belongings.

Now here's another thing that would go in any life story about me: *What Cal Lavender's brain is thinking often doesn't match what her mouth is saying.* For example, when Whitney pulled out the empty top drawer of the dresser, I was thinking: *Why are you showing this to me since anyone with any eyes can see that I don't have any personal belongings to store and Betty is coming for me anyway?*

What I said was "Hmmm. Empty."

Then Whitney took me by the hand and conducted a very detailed, guided tour of her own dresser, which had six overstuffed drawers with all sorts of shirts and underwear hanging out. Plus there was a whole collection of fossilized Bazooka stuck to the side. Very tasty. She held up a smelly old cloth dog with a chewed-up tail. "See this?" she said. "Stole it from my second fosters. Served them right."

I noticed her looking hard at me, probably waiting for me to ask naively, *Fosters? Do you mean The Fosters Freeze downtown?* But Cal Lavender has certainly been around enough to know that she meant a foster home, and I don't like people thinking I haven't been around, so I pointed to the cracked flowerpot on her dresser. "Stolen from a *foster home,* too?" I asked.

"You bet," she said. "Fourth fosters. I call them my souvenirs. Get it? Souvenirs?"

I picked up an old mayonnaise jar filled with leaves. "What's this?"

"Give that back!" She grabbed it out of my hands.

"Sorry," I said, annoyed. "What is it anyway?"

"That's the home of Ike Eisenhower the Fifth."

I knew my history. "Eisenhower? The former president of the United States?"

"What are you talking about?" Whitney was tapping on the glass with her fingernail, which definitely needed cutting. "Ike Eisenhower the Fifth's my pet pill bug. He's named after my favorite candy, Mike and Ike. I made up the last name. Came to me like that." She snapped her fingers.

"Like that?" I asked suspiciously. "Tell me that you never heard of Ike Eisenhower."

"Nope," she stated flatly, then she said, "Mike the Fifth died."

"Mike?"

"Ike's brother. Now it's just Ike the Fifth and me, together since I came to this fosters. How many fosters for you? Does your mother have funny eyebrows, too? I'm ten, but I look eight, which is a good thing 'cause when people are looking for kids to adopt, the younger the better, and I'm plenty young-looking, so I still have a chance. What do you think about spaghetti? I hate spaghetti."

"I'm eleven," I said proudly. "Actually, eleven and one month. But I'm very mature for my age."

She studied me. "Yeah, I figured. Are you at that hormonal age yet?"

I was not about to discuss my personal hormonal situation with a perfect stranger, so I changed the subject. "Is this room always a mess like this?"

She scanned my face like I was talking a foreign language. "We just cleaned yesterday."

She had to be kidding, or blind. When Whitney's life story is written, it will definitely say: *When it comes to slobs, Whitney takes the cake! And her bed is full of it!* Crumbs and gum wrappers and dirty socks. She didn't even seem to notice. How could someone not notice sunflower-seed shells on her pillow?

And I have to say that my other roommate, Amber, was not much better in the cleanliness department. I haven't mentioned that Amber was in the room this whole time, but I guess it's an easy thing to overlook. Amber was by far the quietest person I had ever met in my life, except maybe for Betty when she slid into one of her ultraquiet moods. Amber wasn't politely quiet. She was creepy quiet. The whole time, she sat on her bed looking that *I can see inside of you* look at me, while Whitney did enough talking for both of them.

Within a half hour of being her official temporary roommate, I heard the full and complete list of all the awful, no good, rotten, miserable things that had ever happened to Whitney.

1. Born with a hole in her heart.
2. Fought off death during the surgery to repair the above-mentioned hole. "Yep," she told me, "I heard the doctor say in a real sad voice, 'Too bad. She's dead.' But then I decided, *That's a lie. Whitney, you're not the type to die.*"
3. Kicked out of first fosters. Doesn't know why.

4. Recurring nosebleeds.
5. Almost adopted except lady and man decided they wanted a boy.
6. Head lice and chicken pox at the same time.
7. Kicked out of second fosters 'cause family moved to Alaska.
8. Stuffed into a clothes dryer by other kids at third fosters.
9. Bitten by parrot at this same fosters.
10. Food poisoning on her eighth birthday.
11. Front teeth knocked out in a bike accident and hasn't gotten real fake ones yet.
12. Almost adopted again but lady got cancer and died.
13. Doesn't like to talk about what happened at fourth fosters.
14. Dropped on head by Santa at a group-home Christmas party.

I made a mental note—*Ask Whitney how she got into foster homes in the first place*—but it had to remain a mental note. She didn't stop talking long enough and everything she said came out in one uninterruptible exhale—

"Poisoneddroppedsplitinhalfandmadewholeagain! I have one word to say about that fourth fosters. Messed up, awful, polluted, hellhole, sicko!"

"Whitney, that's six words," I managed to point out.

"Well, la-de-dah. Who cares about numbers? If they ever try to put you in that fosters, you should run away. Remember that!"

"How many fosters have you *been* in, Whitney?" I asked.

"Nine? Ten? I don't know. I lost count."

I know that some people might find it hard to believe that anyone wouldn't know exactly how many different houses they've lived in. But this was something that I could definitely relate to because of all the times that Betty and I just picked up in the middle of the day or night and decided to change addresses. So if anyone had asked me how many places I had lived, how many different schools I had gone to since kindergarten, I would have given the same answer as Whitney: "I lost count."

All the time we were talking—or all the time that Whitney was talking—Amber still had not yet said a word, which, as I said before, was giving me the creeps. One of the things that I've learned by changing schools a million times is how to work my way into a new group of kids. Teachers have always written on my report cards: *Cal Lavender knows how to make herself feel right at home and can make others feel welcome, too.* So even though I was the new kid, I felt responsible for getting Amber involved in the conversation. I tried my best. "What about you, Amber?"

Silence.

"Um, have you been in a lot of um, er, fosters?"

Whitney answered for her. "Yeah, she's been in tons. Even more than me."

I wondered if maybe Amber didn't speak because she *couldn't* speak. Which—because of the logical way that my mind works—reminded me of my mother's friend Harry who had a hole the size of a quarter cut right into his throat. He didn't speak much either. Just the thought of him made me shudder. And since Whitney had been born with an extra hole in one of *her* essential organs, I thought this would be an interesting item of conversation for all of us. I said, "This man I know has a hole in his throat."

"So?" Whitney said sharply.

"He can light up a cigarette and smoke it, not through his mouth like an ordinary person, but through the hole." I held two fingers together, then pressed them to my throat. I made a drawing-in sound that made the inside of my cheeks vibrate.

"Puff, puff," I said. "I swear, you can see smoke and everything."

To me, this was about as fascinating as a conversation could get. So it startled me when Whitney snapped, "Who cares? Anybody can have a hole in their throat."

Any other eleven-year-old girl would have gotten snappy right back. But I tactfully changed the topic. "So Whitney, when are you going back to your real home?"

A look like she had been slapped passed across her

face. She ignored my question and continued in an extremely bratty way, "I bet you think you're going home tomorrow."

"Of course I'm not going home tomorrow," I said. "I'm going home tonight."

What I was thinking was: *I need to go home because if I'm not there, things will "go to hell in a handbasket," as Betty always says. The medicine! Who will make Betty take her medicine? And what will she eat? And who will make sure she gets to the Laundromat? Walking around in dirty underwear is no way for a person to walk around!*

That's what I was thinking, but I said, "Betty's coming for me any time now."

Whitney snorted. "Fat chance. You may talk in perfect complete sentences, but you don't know squat. You're going to be here for a long time."

"No, I'm not," I said.

"A long, *long* time!"

"No!"

"A long, long, *long* time."

By this point, we were glaring at each other, arms crossed against our chests as though we were tied up in knots. There was no reason to believe someone as stupid and rude and messy as Whitney. Why would I believe someone like that? I turned to Amber, hoping that she would shake her head or give some sign that I was right. But without eyebrows to go up and down, her face remained expressionless. It was impossible to know what she was thinking. *If* she was thinking. I guess eyebrows are like street signs. You never know how important they are until they're missing.

But who cared about what Amber was thinking? I didn't need Amber. Or Whitney. I was going home any minute now.

CHAPTER 5

Cal Lavender looks truth square in the eye. I'd be the first to admit that Betty wasn't always the most reliable person in the world. There was the time she went to get popcorn in the movies and decided that she just wasn't in the mood to sit still and didn't remember to come back until I had seen the same picture three times straight through. But forget about me all night? Leave me stranded in an orange-colored house with strangers? Never!

At 8:30, I joined the lineup of girls outside the bathroom, getting ready for bed. While we waited for Amber to finish up inside, Monica tossed a pencil down the hallway. Whitney got down on her hands and knees, crawled after it, and brought it back in her mouth for Monica to throw again. Fern thought this childish doggie behavior was the funniest thing ever. I ignored them. I most especially ignored Whitney.

At 8:35, I brushed my teeth and washed my face.

At 8:50, I put on the nightgown the Knitting Lady handed me. It was a nice soft cotton with kittens on it that I might have liked under different circumstances.

At 8:53, I pulled back the sheets and blanket and got into bed. Whitney kept making *la-de-dah* faces at me, but I'm good at ignoring annoying people.

At 8:55, I got out of bed and changed back into my clothes. I folded the blanket and then the nightgown into two tidy packages. I sat on the edge of the cot, my hands folded on my lap.

When the Knitting Lady sat next to me on the bed, I glanced out of the corner of my eye and could see that she looked worried. I thought, *You don't have to worry about Cal Lavender. I can take care of myself, thank you very much.*

I said . . . nothing. I stared past her and put all my focus on the flowered wallpaper.

"H-hey," she said. "Having trouble settling in?"

I gave my chin a stiff shake. "Betty is coming any minute. It's pointless for me to get into bed."

The Knitting Lady started to say something, but Whitney the Interrupter interrupted. "You're the pointless one. You don't get the point! This is a group home. Parents never, ever come at night to pick up their kid."

That was it! I whirled around to face her. "You don't know what Betty will do!"

"They won't let her come! That's the law!"

"Who's *they?* What law? You don't know what's going to happen!"

The Knitting Lady's voice was soft and firm at the same time: "Whitney, Cal's right. We never know from one minute to the next what will happen. Do we, Cal?"

"That's right," I said. "She doesn't know anything."

"N-none of us know. Anything can happen. What about a compromise? You go to sleep. And if your mother comes tonight—"

"*When* my mother comes," I said.

"I'll wake you. P-promise."

"No," I said. "I'll wait up."

"Let her learn the hard way," Whitney said.

The Knitting Lady shot her a look, which I was glad to see. "That's enough now, Whitney. You more than anyone know how hard the first night is." And then she turned back to me, and I guess she was having one of her system overloads because she really started stumbling over her words: "T-take your time. Sit up awhile. If you n-need anything, I'm-m—"

"I'm just fine!" I blurted out. Her stuttering was making me even more impatient. I know it was impolite, but I couldn't sit there waiting for her to say what she was trying to say. I didn't need anything from her. I just wanted to get out of this place.

When the Knitting Lady stood, I felt the bed tip slightly. I heard the click of the overhead light. Thank goodness she was gone. Darkness fell around me. There was the sound of slow, steady footsteps as the Knitting Lady walked down the stairs. I listened to Fern's giggling coming through the wall. Monica was whining about something. A toilet flushed. I could hear Whitney chewing gum in bed and the crinkle-crinkle noises of Amber's sheets as she tossed around.

And I waited. I waited for Betty to charge in Betty-style and rescue me. As I waited, I tried to draw calmness from all the sounds—the chewing, the tossing, the flushing—but all I could think was *Now!*

Now! Now! Now! Now! Now! Now! Now! Now! Now! Now! Now! Now! Now! Now! Now! Now! Now! Now! Now! Now! Now! Now! Now! Now! Now!

Betty is coming for me NOW! She is!

And then two more ice ages passed, and a whole flood of thoughts came at me: *Betty is lost. Of course, she's lost! Betty can't do anything without me. She's wandering the streets, not knowing what bus to take, whether to go left or right, north or south. Or maybe she's hurt. That's it! Horrible things happen all the time to people, and Betty is never, ever careful enough. A car ran a red light and hit her. She was bitten by a rat, fell down a long flight of steps, was run over by a garbage truck. Maybe Betty is dead.*

I pictured her in a coffin, her hands resting lightly on her chest. There would be makeup on her face because that's what they do with dead people. They put makeup all over them so that they don't look so dead. I saw that in a movie once. Betty would hate that. She hates makeup when she's living, and she'd really hate it when she's dead. She'd never stand for it. Never!

So maybe she isn't dead. Maybe . . . maybe . . . maybe it's something worse.

A dread, something even more horrible than the thought of Betty in a coffin, started at the base of my spine and slithered its way to the top of my head. I couldn't let myself think what I was starting to think. I couldn't think it. I couldn't!

Then I thought it: *Betty isn't dead. Betty isn't lost. Betty isn't here because she doesn't want to be here.*

It felt like someone stuck a vacuum cleaner hose down my throat and sucked my heart right up out of me.

I suddenly felt more tired than I had ever been in my entire life. Every muscle gave up at once. My stomach hurt something awful. It took every bit of energy I had left to crawl beneath the blanket. I turned my face into the pillow and held it there. There was a smell I didn't recognize. It wasn't my smell. It wasn't Betty's smell. I guess it was the smell of every kid who had ever wound up in this bed.

I guess maybe I started to cry.

"Cal, are you crying?" It was Whitney's voice.

"No," I said. My jaw was quivering from the strain of holding it in. "I never cry."

"Good. Because I can't invite a crybaby for a sleep-over. My bed would get wet."

I lifted my face from the pillow and looked across the narrow gulf that separated our beds. When I saw Whitney reach across to touch my mattress, I let my right hand drop over the side. She fumbled and took it in hers. Whitney's hand was soft and as light as a piece of paper. And she was grinning, her two big glinting silver front teeth catching the sliver of streetlight that was peeking in through the blinds. That did something to me. It made me feel better somehow, like there were two glowing lights so that I wouldn't have to be all alone in the dark.

"But Betty doesn't let me have sleepovers," I whispered.

"Come on! Don't be so goody-goody. Betty's not here now!" She held open her blanket. Why not? After a slight hesitation, I scooted into the tent of it. I was surrounded by the smell of sunflower seeds and dirty socks and, beneath it, what I would come to recognize as a distinctive Whitney smell. I whispered, "Whitney, is your mom coming for you, too?"

"Nah," she said. "Don't have one."

"No mom?"

There was a long silence. Then, "I got a different kind of mom. A dead one."

I felt another shiver go through me, and I didn't have a clue of what to say to that. "I'm sorry" didn't feel right, and asking questions didn't feel right either. Luckily, I didn't have to say anything because Whitney bolted upright. "Hey, Knitting Lady. Don't worry. She didn't take off. She's in here with me."

I peeked out of the blanket and saw the short silhouette framed in the doorway.

"No one's sleepy in here yet," Whitney went on. "Right, Cal?" Then she knocked on the wall—three short, quick knocks; a pause, then two more.

It must have been their secret code because Monica and Fern came rushing in and threw themselves on my now-empty bed. Monica immediately started whining, "Stop it, Fern. Your feet are in my face. It's not fair."

"Whose bed is this?" Fern asked.

"The new girl."

"The new girl? There's a new girl? Oh, I forgot! The new girl."

I waited for the Knitting Lady to order us all back into our own beds. But instead, she asked, "Well girls, if you're not sleepy, what do you have in mind?"

Whitney started butt-bumping the mattress. "You know!"

"I d-do? Cal, do you have a clue as to what she's talking about?"

"Me? How would I know?"

Monica switched on a small lamp. The room glowed with warm light. She said to the Knitting Lady, "Why do you always do that? Pretend you don't know what we want?"

And then Whitney said to me, "She tells the world's best stories. But she makes us beg first."

The Knitting Lady laughed. "You girls have really got my number! Is there any particular story you want to hear?"

There was some movement behind me, which made me jump. Once again, I had forgotten all about Amber being in the room. Her bed squeaked when she got out and walked to her dresser. She reached into the top drawer and pulled out something that was dangling from a long chain.

"Oh, *that* story," the Knitting Lady said, sounding surprised but somehow not surprised at all. "Aren't you tired of that story yet? N-no, of course you're not tired of it. Truth is, I never get tired of telling it."

So Amber got back into bed. Monica and Fern curled up against each other, hooked together like snails.

"The s-story of Amber," the Knitting Lady began. "A valuable jewel that was born out of destruction.

CHAPTER 6

"Picture a long time ago," the Knitting Lady continued. "There was a storm. Amber was born from this—low-pressure zones that had built up over time and space."

"I have a question already," I said.

"G-go ahead, Cal."

"I don't understand."

"What part?"

"This story. Is this about Amber—her?" I pointed to the girl.

Whitney snorted. "Man-oh-man, that's like a dumb question Fern would ask. It's about a rock. A rock! Amber, show her."

Amber held up the necklace that she had taken from her dresser. Dangling from the chain was a polished orange-yellow nugget cradled in a cobweb of silver.

The Knitting Lady nodded in agreement and said, "That's amber. But Cal's question is actually quite a good one. Hold on to that question as I tell the story. So, where was I? The storm. It was a humdinger. Picture a tree in the midst of it. This wasn't a very big tree. In fact, it was little more than a sapling."

"Oh, the poor tree," Monica said. "I'm glad I'm not the tree. I'd be *soooo* scared."

Whitney nudged me and rolled her eyes. "She says that every time. She's scared of everything!"

"Well, I *would* be scared," Monica insisted.

"B-being scared is nothing to be ashamed of. Everyone gets scared in scary situations. We each learn to handle frightening things in our own way. This tree had been through so many storms, it had learned to be very flexible, to bend and sway in order to survive. But not—"

"Not in this storm," Whitney interrupted.

"T-true. This storm proved too much for it. Its bark was no more protection than lace. Leaves blew to kingdom come. Can you hear the branches of this young tree snap with a sickening crack?" The Knitting Lady gave her hands one loud clap.

Fern started giggling. "Why are you laughing?" I asked.

"Don't ask. Fern's always laughing, except when she's crying," Whitney said.

Monica took a sharp inhale of breath. "This next part is so scary. I don't like this part."

"Man-oh-man, Monica, you are such a wimp," Whitney said. "You always—"

"Wh-Whitney, you know how this story goes. What happens next?"

"And then, the plunderers and marauders came forth!" she recited.

"Exactly! W-when the bark broke, it was like skin splitting. Everything underneath—the bones of the tree, its fragile inside, its delicate heart—became vulnerable. Then an army of insects, parasites, and diseases marched forth with their pinching jaws and big appetites. They seemed unstoppable. What could the tree do?"

"I'd run," Monica said. "I'd get out of there so fast!"

Whitney said sarcastically, "Man-oh-man, Monica, you can't even walk a half a block without dying of heat frustration."

"Heat prostration," I corrected.

"Heat *is* frustrating," Monica moaned. "I die from the heat."

"Where's Monica walking?" Fern asked.

"Jeez-Louise, not Monica," Whitney said.

I wanted them all to be quiet so that I could hear the rest of the story, so I took it upon myself to sort things out for them. I said to Fern, "To begin with, Monica's not going anywhere." Then I pointed out to Monica, "And secondly, a tree is rooted to the ground. It can't just pick itself up and run."

Whitney said, "Hey, I never asked this before. Did the

tree try yelling for help? If it was me, I'd be screaming my head off."

"Trees can't yell," I said. "That's just not logical."

"It doesn't have to be logical! It's a story. Animals can talk. Trees can yell. So did it? Yell, I mean."

"P-perhaps it did try. Y-yes, I know it did. But unfortunately, it spoke a special tree language that no one understood. Or maybe no one believed. Not many people pay much attention to the complaints of young trees. So next— That's right, Whitney. You know."

"It found a way to protect itself!" she said.

"What a clever w-weapon it found. That young hurting tree went deep within itself and discovered a steady flowing fountain of resin."

"Resin. That's the same as pancake syrup," Whitney tried to inform me, but I informed her, "I know what resin is. But how can that be a weapon?"

"G-good question, Cal. This resin had a sharp, pungent smell. Big globs oozed out of the tree's wounds. Those plunderers and marauders didn't know what hit them! Some hightailed it away as fast as possible. The slower villains thought, *My-oh-my, what is that mouthwatering smell?* But their first taste was their last because they found themselves trapped in a flypaper of syrup."

Fern waved her hand in the air. "Another question!"

"Y-yes, Fern?"

"Are we?"

"Are we what?"

"Having pancakes for breakfast tomorrow morning?"

"Ignore her," Whitney said. "Get to the next part—the part where the sap hardened!"

"R-right! The resin hardened, trapping all the villains and sealing the wound of the tree. Over time, the sap continued to harden. The shell grew thicker and more impenetrable. That's amber. Nothing can get in and nothing can get out."

"The end," Whitney announced.

"So when did all this happen?" Fern asked.

Monica rubbed her eyes and yawned. "Fern, you've heard this story a million times. It happened about a million years ago."

Whitney spoke directly to me: "See? I told you she tells a good story. Her stuttering doesn't wreck it at all."

My eyes darted to the Knitting Lady and back. "Whitney, that's incredibly rude."

"But it's true. If something's true, it can't be rude, right? And *she* doesn't mind." She addressed the Knitting Lady. "You don't mind, right?"

The Knitting Lady didn't answer, but you could see that it didn't bother her a bit. "A-Amber, what do you see when you hold up your necklace? That's right. Tilt it so that the light is to your advantage. What do you see inside?"

I twisted around. I was very interested in hearing her

answer, but even more I wanted to hear her voice. Maybe it would be squeaky. Maybe she would have some kind of accent. I waited. But Amber remained silent and held the necklace out in my direction.

"Me?" I asked, and she nodded.

"Go on," Whitney urged.

I walked to her bed, and, when I took the jewel, Amber watched me carefully, as though I might never give it back. I held it to the light. "Something in there looks like a bug!"

"It *is* a bug!" said the Knitting Lady.

"I hate bugs!" Monica said.

"You like Ike, right? So, don't be a baby," Whitney said. "It can't hurt you."

"That's r-right. It's probably a termite that was stopped cold in the act of destroying the tree. There are also things in there too small to see, like bacteria. So much dangerous debris of the past, but all trapped safely inside. None of those old hurts are a problem anymore."

～

That night, I was allowed to sleep in Whitney's bed. Fern and Monica took over mine. "A real sleepover," the Knitting Lady said. "One night only."

A minute after the lights went out, Whitney's body jolted and went still. I never thought anyone could fall asleep as fast as that. It was like she had been unplugged.

Her breathing lengthened. It turned so quiet that it worried me. I kept putting my ear to her back to make sure her breath was still there.

Pretty soon, Fern was snoring slightly. Monica mumbled a few words. She was already dreaming. But I still wasn't anywhere near ready to sleep.

I wondered what Betty was doing. She can't fall asleep unless I talk her to sleep.

I wondered: *Why is Monica so scared of everything? Why does Fern laugh at everything?*

What did the Knitting Lady mean: We each handle scary things in our own way?

Was I supposed to make my own breakfast?

What did Whitney's scar feel like? Was it rough and even, like a zipper to her heart?

What if I *never* fell asleep?

I wondered: *What was the Knitting Lady's story really about?*

And still, I was awake. I thought of the other things that might have been trapped inside of amber. Seeds and feathers and molecules of air from another era. It wasn't until I started thinking about what melted amber would look like, imagining it turning to liquid gold, that I started drifting off. I hopped on a million-year-old bubble of air and the next thing I knew, it was morning.

CHAPTER 7

Sunlight was pouring in on me. I couldn't tell where I was, what day, what planet I had landed on. I felt like I weighed nothing in all that light. Out of habit, I reached over, patted the space next to me, felt nothing. No Betty!

A voice said: "Man-oh-man, what is that mouthwatering smell?"

What? Plunderers and marauders! Termites trapped in amber! Was I dreaming?

I bolted upright. I was in a bed. A girl—I remembered now, *that* girl, Whitney—was sitting in the middle of the room, tearing through a pile of clothes. Without glancing at me, she said, "Cal, breakfast! Smells like pancakes and resin," then pulled off her pajama top—that scar again!— and put on a wrinkled shirt.

She asked, "Wanna play cards later?"

My brain felt fuzzy, which most definitely is not the usual state of my brain. "Cards?"

"You know." She made a motion like she was dealing. "Wanna play?"

"Sure," I said. "Why not?"

"Good. Because when I'm done with you, your life won't be worth a penny."

☙

I, Cal Lavender, was definitely not myself. A fuzz brain, crying and whiny the night before. Definitely not me. But after I brushed my teeth, checked the mirror, and adjusted My Face for Unbearably Unpleasant and Embarrassing Situations, I felt more myself. Or at least as close to myself as an eleven-year-old can be when she is being forced to live not her real life.

So.

On the first morning of not really living my story, Fern and Amber had pancake-making duty. Now, I know how to make pancakes. You can count on any pancakes made by Cal Lavender to be light and fluffy the way Betty and I like them. But the way the others attacked the tall stack made by Fern and Amber, you'd think they actually liked their pancakes to have the taste and texture of a sponge. Well, there's no accounting for taste, as Betty always says.

After eating, we were all supposed to pitch in and clean up. That seemed fair enough to me, but everyone else complained their heads off, especially Monica. Because of the cast on her arm, she got to do just about nothing, but still she whined.

"I *caaaan't* wipe down the table."

And, "My arm itches *soooo* much."

And, "I'm tired. Fern snored all night."

And, "Whitney is being mean to me. She called me a big baby."

At first, I got drying duty and Whitney got to wash. As you can imagine, she did not do an acceptable job. I had to keep handing back the dishes because she never got off all the suds.

After her fifteenth unacceptable dish, she snapped at me, "Okay, then. You wash! I'll dry!" But then she also got snippy because each time I handed her a knife to dry, I yelled "Sharp!" which to my way of thinking is a very safety-conscious thing to do.

When the kitchen was finally clean, all of us—minus the Knitting Lady—went into Talk Central and started watching a monster movie on TV. Every time the vampire came on screen and bared his blood-dripping fangs, Whitney yelled "Sharp!" Fern thought that that was hysterical, and pretty soon she and Monica were also yelling "Sharp!" Maybe it was a little funny the first time, but by the hundredth time, there was no humor left at all.

So immature!

At the first commercial, Monica made us change the channel because the movie was getting too scary for her. Nothing else remotely interesting was on. Then we helped the Knitting Lady with the laundry, only I didn't have any laundry. Still, I was the only one who didn't act as though helping was the end of the world.

After laundry, I played blackjack with Whitney. She wasn't as good as she had bragged about. As I suspected, I was a much better counter. I usually get straight A's in math, even when Betty moves me to a new school in the middle of the term. Right in the middle of the game, right when I was about to wipe her out of cards, Whitney made a big announcement: "It's time to educate Cal."

I couldn't imagine what *she* had to teach *me,* since I was winning just about every hand. Still, I followed her upstairs to the bedroom. It was just the two of us. She got all mysterious, locked the door, and told me to listen very, very carefully.

Let it be known: Cal Lavender is a very, very good listener.

According to Whitney, this was not just an ordinary house I had landed in; it was a whole world that was nothing like my old world.

"Orange is just the tick of the iceberg," she said.

"Tip," I corrected.

"Tick," she insisted. "If you don't understand what's going on, man-oh-man, you're going to be ticked-off 24/7."

My new world, she explained, has its own language, secret codes, and horror stories. She said, "You need to know who's who and what's what, or it's— What's it for you?" She made a slicing motion across her neck.

"Curtains?" I said.

"Yeah, curtains for you."

I said, "You make it sound like I'm in one of those lost civilizations on the Discovery Channel. Why do I have to know anything? I'm only here by mistake."

She was eating sunflower seeds at the time and making a pile of the shells on her bed. "That's what"—*crack, crack*—"every new kid thinks at first." *Crack, crack.*

"What does everyone think?"

"That they're here by mistake." *Crack-crack.* "The crybabies are the ones who drive me crazy. Don't even"—*crack*—"get me started on the crybabies."

"You mean like Monica?" I asked.

"Not Monica! Monica's a whiner. The crybabies are new kids who"—*crack*—"say they don't"—*crack*—"care where they live, but they sweat a lot, which is"—*crack, crack*—"how you can tell they're"—*crack*—"scared to death." *Crack!*

"Could you *please* stop that?" I put my hands over my ears.

"The sunflower seeds?"

"Yes! No! Yes, the seeds! Not just the seeds. Stop acting like I'm everyone else. Like I'm going to be here forever."

"Well, maybe not forever." *Crack.* "But you're going to be here longer than you"—*crack*—"think. Everyone is. So you might as well know what's what. To start with"—*crack*—"you should know that you're a Code 300 kid."

"What's that?"

"It means you're not a Code 600 kid."

"That's great, Whitney. Very helpful."

She missed the sarcasm. "Thanks. I mean to be helpful. And you should know about the social worker. It's a good news/bad news situation. Which first?"

"Good."

"The good thing is that everyone here has the same social worker, so I can tell you everything you need to know and save you from learning the hard way. The bad news is that when you see her, you're going to ask yourself: *Man-oh-man, is that animal, vegetable, or mineral?* You *do* know what a social worker is, right? If you don't, it's nothing to burn in shame about."

Did she think I was an idiot? "Of course, I know. I already have a social worker. I mean, Betty does. That's who gives us our food stamps and—"

"Not *that* kind! A special *kid* social worker just for you. Her name is Mrs. S-something-long-in-the-middle-that-no-one-can-pronounce-with-*ski*-at-the-end, so everyone just calls her Mrs. S. There's something you got to know about her."

"What?" I asked. Only I guess I had the wrong tone of voice because Whitney snapped, "Don't get la-de-dah again! This is important information. It isn't for babies. Are you listening?"

I blinked once.

"Well, are you?"

"Yes!"

"Good. Because this is reality TV, starring guess who."

"Who?"

"You!" she said in exasperation. "Now, about Mrs. S. The big thing is to always be super-polite. Don't get pissed off and spit in her eye because Mrs. S. has the power to get you in and out of certain foster homes. Take it from me personally, it doesn't pay to spit in her eye." Whitney took measure of me. "You won't have any trouble with sucking up. You have the la-de-dah act down pat. Now, quiz time. You have a choice between being on the bad side of Mrs. S. or diving into a pit of hot lava. Which do you choose?"

"Mrs. S."

"No! No! No! What do you choose?"

"Hot lava?" I answered hesitantly.

"Right. I could tell that you were smart! Now you're learning!"

That was just the start of my first educational session. That day in the Pumpkin House, I also learned the following:

1. The social worker—the dreaded Mrs. S.—would help decide when and whether I could go back home with Betty again.

2. Whitney and Amber had their parental ties severed, which sounded to me like something out of a horror movie, with a parent sliced away and rolling down a flight of stairs like a decapitated head. But Whitney explained that it's the opposite of a horror show. It means that they can both be adopted as soon as the perfect new parents are found for them.

3. Flush the downstairs toilet after every pee or it over-flows.

4. Code 300 kids are the ones who had something wrong done to them (or have a mother who has episodes). Code 600 kids are the cold-blooded killer/arsonist/drug-dealer types who are locked up in kid jail.

5. Fern didn't have her parental ties severed, which means that she gets to go home and live with her mother sometimes. She loves going home. Only something bad always happens and she has to come back into foster care.

6. Ditto with Monica.

7. Amber doesn't have cancer, which is what I first thought. It turns out that she has this nervous prob-lem and, when her nerves kick up, she actually pulls out her hair. "*Ouch* is right," Whitney said. "She doesn't do it on purpose or anything. It's all in her head. And her noggin. Her brain, too."

8. The Knitting Lady won't let me call Betty no matter how much I beg. So don't beg.

"I know this isn't the easiest stuff to have dumped on you all at once," Whitney said. "I bet you want to run off somewhere and puke."

"I'm fine," I said quickly. "So out of all that, what's the *most* important thing to know?"

She thought for a moment. "You know the expression 'God helps those who . . . who . . .' Who does God help?"

I nodded eagerly. "Who help themselves!" I was very good at helping myself.

"Yeah, that's what I mean. Only, don't count on that to work around here. Everything gets decided behind your back, and there's not much you can do about it."

CHAPTER 8

Later that first day, the Knitting Lady told us to get ready for a short road trip. "We have things to do!"

Transportation was an old-model van with all sorts of dents and bruises. Since the paint was peeled off and faded, there was no way to tell the original color. Maybe it was once orange like the house. Only now it was somewhere between puke green and dog-poop brown. But as long as it didn't have a siren and something embarrassing written along the side like "Pathetic Group-Home Girls," dog poop–puke brown-green was okay with me. Cal Lavender is no snob when it comes to minivans. I'm more of a public-transportation type of individual.

Since I was the new girl, I got to sit up front, which made Monica start whining. "I get carsick in the back. I *do*! Don't blame me if I puke. It feels like a million degrees in here."

I rolled down the window. Then it felt like a million degrees minus one. But I didn't care. I was getting out. That's another way that Betty and I are exactly alike. Don't fence us in! I felt like one of those dogs you see in the back of pickup trucks, her head tilted up, her mouth open and trying to swallow as much fresh air as she can.

The Knitting Lady looked pretty funny in the driver's seat. She was one of those gray-haired ladies that you see driving down the road, her head barely clearing the steering wheel. From the back, I bet it looked like the van was driving itself. Her feet didn't even reach the pedals, so everything she needed was right there on the dash. That was very interesting to me, since I had never seen anything like that before. She pushed a button, pulled a lever, and we were off.

"There! Look there!" Unfortunately, Whitney was sitting directly behind me, cracking sunflower seeds, yelling in my ear, and kicking me in the bottom through the seat. "Mountain Mike's Pizza. Nobody here likes pepperoni. Do you?"

When I didn't respond immediately, she kicked harder. "Pepperoni? Do you?" And when we drove by a rec center, she jabbed me in the shoulder. "That's where the pool is. Did I tell you about the pool yet? It's gotta be the best pool ever. Man-oh-man, you have to take a test before they let you in the deep part, so now I'm taking swim lessons. I didn't want to take swim lessons, not because I'm scared or anything and— Look! That's Horace Mann Middle School. Memorize that! *Horace. Mann. Middle. School.* We all walk together."

She reached over and tapped the Knitting Lady's

shoulder—"She's in sixth, right?"—then tapped me—
"You didn't flunk or anything, right?"—then poked
Monica—"She'll walk with us, right? And eat lunch with
us, right? Everything together, right?"

I did not say anything, but I was thinking: *Wrong!*
This is July, and there is no way that I will still be living
not-my-real-life when school starts. No way.

Besides, if I did have to go to a school, it would certainly not be *that* one. As we drove by, I saw that Horace
Mann was mostly a cluster of portables surrounding the
main building, which to me looked like a very bad school.
Perhaps the worst school that ever existed. I thought: *Not*
that it matters because I won't go there. And even if I did
have to go there—which definitely is not going to happen—
maybe I would walk with them sometimes, but there is no
way that I would do everything with them. I would have
to make it very clear very quickly that Cal Lavender is
never joined at the hip with anyone. I am an extremely
independent type of person.

Whitney kicked again: "Everything together? Right?"

౿

Whitney had told me so many things that day, I could not
believe that she had forgotten one of the most important.
I would have to get examined by the nurse from the
Department of Children's Services. No kid ever got out of

it. That was our first stop of the day. Everyone else got to stay in the waiting room, playing with little-kid toys and eating junk from the vending machine, while I followed Nurse Francine. That's what her name tag said. *Nurse Francine.* She led me into an examination room and asked, "So?"

I said, "I'm not the type to get sick. Put that down on my chart."

Nurse Francine bent her head and took my blood pressure. I had never met anyone who talked only in questions. First, she shoved a tongue depressor far down my throat, and, while I was gagging, she asked, "Make you gag?" She pulled out my eyelids by the eyelashes and shined a light onto the inner linings. Then came other questions, strange, embarrassing ones that she asked in a flat, bored voice. "Do you currently have diarrhea? Do you have itching in your vaginal area? Do you ever wet the bed? Do you ever hear voices?"

"No!" I said, outraged. "No diarrhea. No itching. No wetting. No voices."

Then she picked up a clipboard and began turning pages. Her hands were a whirl. "How are you feeling in general?"

That was the first question she asked that I actually had to stop and think about. I was feeling . . . ? How? There must have been ten thousand words for what I was feeling. Words for missing Betty. Words for wondering when I could go home. Is that what she wanted?

I suddenly suspected that without a doubt this must be a trick question. If I answered wrong, a trapdoor was going to spring open beneath my feet—whoosh!—and suck me away someplace where Betty would never find me.

I, Cal Lavender, who never, ever felt nervous, measured every word. "I feel . . . I feel . . ." I looked at my feet. "I feel full of feelings."

Nurse Francine's face dropped and she lowered her eyes, like she was the one who was embarrassed instead of me. "Hmmmm. Is that so?" She marked something on her clipboard. Was it a black mark? Something that was going to get me in trouble? But when I strained to see it, she flipped my chart closed.

ᴖ

After that, we got back into the van and then stopped at the drugstore to pick up some head lice–treatment shampoo because Nurse Francine said that I had nits, which I certainly did not. And if I did, it must have come from sharing a room with someone who keeps a bug as a pet.

After that, we went grocery shopping, and the Knitting Lady said that, because I was the new girl, I could pick three things that I especially liked or wanted to try.

Whitney kept chanting, "Pop-Tarts, Pop-Tarts, Pop-Tarts." Fern said that maybe she *does* like pepperoni, but she forgets. Maybe it's sausage she doesn't like. Or anchovies. Monica said that she's definitely highly allergic to pepperoni and sausage and anchovies and begged me— "Please, please, please!"—to get plain pizza because that was one of only three things that she could eat without getting a stomachache. The other two things were pancakes and frozen chicken sticks, but only the supermarket generic brand.

I ignored them. Unlike most eleven-year-old girls, I believe in eating nutritionally. Betty is fond of saying, *Your body is your temple,* so I set a good example for the others by filling our cart with lettuce, tomatoes, cucumbers, avocados, mustard, mayonnaise, and tortillas in order to make Cal Lavender's Infinitely Superior Lettuce, Tomato, Cucumber, Avocado, Mustard, and Mayonnaise Tortilla Roll-Ups.

"Very creative," the Knitting Lady said. She clearly approved of my nutritional standards because even though Whitney kept calling avocados "slimy, green fat balls" and Monica was whining, "That's seven things, not three," the Knitting Lady didn't make me put anything back.

⁀

So that was that—the condensed version of the first day of living not really my life. I also came to some specific conclusions about the other girls in the house. That's something else to note in my life story: Cal Lavender can tell everything there is to know about a person within fifteen minutes of meeting them. So without a doubt, I knew that these girls were strange. By this, I mean strange in their own unique way, which is the definition of being truly strange. I've seen plenty of kids who put on a big act of being strange—like dressing gothic or doing something purple with their hair—but then they're all strange in the same way, which makes them not strange at all.

But the girls in the Pumpkin House didn't fall into any of the usual groups. They weren't jocks or math nerds or school-play kids. For example, I can say without a doubt that I have never come across a group for hair-plucking girls.

Later that evening, when the Knitting Lady and I were alone in the kitchen, I brought up this observation. She more or less agreed with my conclusion. She said, "We have our own groups. For example, there are the girls who refuse to think or feel anything bad about their parents, no matter how much their parents disappoint and hurt them."

"How do they do that?" I asked.

"It's quite a trick, all right. Some of these girls get so

silly that there's no space for anything serious. You'd think they didn't have brain or a care in the world. They laugh at anything. Sometimes, they can't stop laughing."

"Fern?" I asked, and the Knitting Lady said, "That's for you to decide. And then, we have girls who can't stand change. They're t-terrified of it. Sound like anyone you know? And I can't forget the runners. They blow out of every foster home, even the good ones."

"Why do they do that?"

"It's c-complicated. Maybe someday you can help me figure that out."

"I'd be very glad to help. I'm good at figuring things out. What about Whitney's group?"

"Some children have been in foster care so long, they know more about the way things work than any social worker. Whitney's something of a genius in that respect, isn't she? Then there are the failure-to-thrive children—"

"Failure to drive?" I asked.

"Thrive," she corrected. "Some girls have such difficult lives that they somehow will themselves to stop growing. Stop *thriving*."

"I don't like the sound of that," I said.

"It's no p-picnic. But you're not that type."

"I'm not any type at all. I don't fit in a group because I don't belong here," I pointed out.

"Ahhhh," the Knitting Lady said. "That's another type."

"What do you mean 'ahhhh'? You say 'ahhhh' a lot."

"I'll tell you a story about it sometime. But the bottom line is that whatever you're thinking, whatever you might be afraid of, whatever you're proud of, you, Cal Lavender, are far from being alone."

CHAPTER 9

The second day of *not really my life* was the hottest day in the history of the universe. We were all in Talk Central, all moping around except Whitney. While we moped, she danced, skipped, and swirled, the same bouncing rubber band–ball girl no matter what the weather. She insisted that we play AA, her all-time favorite game. *AA* happens to stand for "Alcoholics Anonymous," which is a club that grown-ups go to in order to help them stop drinking. I could tell that Monica and Fern already knew about AA the way some kids know about PTA meetings. They didn't come out and say so, but I concluded that their parents stopped going to meetings, which was part of the reason why they now had to live in a group home.

Whitney was tapping her right foot, waiting for us to give her our full attention. "My name is Whitney P.," she said. "This is my first time here."

Of course, it wasn't her first time. It was just part of the game to say so. I caught on quickly and said, "Hi, Whitney!" when everyone else did. I think we were supposed to have tons of warm enthusiasm, only our "Hi,

Whitney" came out limp because of the heat that I already mentioned.

Whitney gave us a disappointed and annoyed look, but continued anyway. "I am"—*dramatic pause*—"an alcoholic." She pressed her hands to her heart. "It all started way back when I was born with a big old hole in my heart. *Not* in my throat, which is something any old Harry in the street can have and is nothing to brag about. And if that's not enough, well, man-oh-man, there were plenty other things that ran wild in my life. To begin with . . ."

Whitney then provided us with her usual rundown of the awful, no good, rotten, miserable things that have happened to her and then threw in some other juicy tidbits, which were more or less a pack of lies. I have to admit that Whitney was a pretty entertaining reforming alcoholic. When she got to the end and was crying fake tears, she reminded us that we were all supposed to start saying peppy AA things like "Thanks for sharing, Whitney!"

However, as I mentioned before, no one was in the mood for peppy. Fern didn't even have the energy to giggle. Monica sunk further into the couch and whined, "Be quiet, Whitney. I have a headache. You're talking too much. You always talk too much."

"Me? Talk too much?" Whitney looked genuinely surprised, then she lashed out. "You snore."

"I don't!" Monica protested. "I just breathe heavy. It's my allergies."

"Nope. You snore." As soon as Whitney started making piggy sounds, that did it. The lid of Pandora's box lifted, which is something that I learned about during Betty's Greek-mythology, library phase. What this means in regular English is that it was as if dozens of mean spirits came screaming out. As the only sensible, polite person in the room, I was the only one who didn't unleash something mean about someone else.

"You smell like armpits."

"Your teeth have green fuzz."

"Stop laughing at everything."

"You stop laughing at me!"

"You'll never be adopted!"

"No, you'll never be adopted!"

"I don't want to be adopted!"

Of course, Amber didn't say anything either. At this point, I had given up any hope of ever hearing her voice. But I could tell the whole scene was making her nervous because she started plucking at the few eyebrow hairs that were still left on her face.

It wasn't shaping up to be a very good day.

The Knitting Lady came into the room then, took a seat next to Amber, and gently sandwiched the girl's hands between her own. The Knitting Lady herself wasn't holding up too well with the weather either. She had cracked lips and instead of looking 111, she looked 112. Even though she was sweating, her lips and teeth started chattering like they belonged to a little kid who had been in the water too long. She was definitely having a bad speaking day.

"S-stop it! S-stop it, already. All this b-bickering and squabbling! If everyone stops c-complaining for ten seconds, I'll tell a story."

Story. That was the magic word.

"A true story!" Whitney demanded.

"All my stories are t-true. They're all about your ancestors."

Whitney took a sharp inhale and then released it through her nose. "I don't have ancestors. That's why I'm here."

"Now, Whitney, why do you think that? You have h-hundreds of ancestors. You all do. I've told you about some of them. Do you know who I mean?"

Monica shrugged.

"H-how about you, Fern?"

"Huh?" she said.

I said, "I don't belong here, so I can't be expected to know."

The Knitting Lady looked disappointed, as if we had let her down in a small but very important way. "S-Superman, for instance. His p-parents couldn't raise him, so some kind earthlings took him in. And what about the story I told you the other day? He's one of your ancestors, too, each and every one of you."

"What story?" Fern asked.

"Basket Boy!" Whitney exclaimed.

"The one adopted by the fairy?" Fern asked.

"Pharaoh," the Knitting Lady corrected.

Whitney was nodding her big head so fast, she looked like a bobble-head doll in the back window of a car. "I knew Basket Boy was my kind of kid! When his mother stuck him in those river reeds, did he scream his head off? No! Did he get all mealymouthed and wimpy around the guy who adopted him? No! Not even when he found out that his new father was king of half the world and everything."

"Th-that's the story I mean! That boy who was put into a basket by his mother went on to greatness. He did amazing things to help his people."

By Basket Boy, I figured that she meant Moses. Betty was a great reader, and as I mentioned before, we spent a lot of time in the public library, studying whatever caught her attention. The Bible happened to be one of Betty's favorites, so I knew all about Moses and how he never lived with his real mother again.

I pointed that out. Then I pointed out that my mother was coming for me any time now. "Therefore," I concluded, "Basket Boy can't be my ancestor, too."

"Are you calling the Knitting Lady a liar?" Whitney challenged.

"No, but—"

"The Knitting Lady makes things up, but she doesn't lie," Monica insisted.

"No, but—"

"Who's a liar?" Fern asked. "Basket Boy?"

I stayed firm. "Nobody's a liar. But the fact is, I'm not going to be adopted. I have a mother."

The Knitting Lady patted Whitney on the shoulder to calm her down, but she talked to me. "I didn't say that you'll never see your m-mother again. Some of our ancestors get adopted, some don't. You still share a common history."

"History?" I asked.

"It means that you have similar experiences. You have some of the same heroes. You know the same stories. You're members of the same tribe."

Whitney looked lost. So did the others. But for me, a thought took shape, and I guess the Knitting Lady caught me thinking it. "Cal, do you see what I'm getting at?"

"Well, if Basket Boy—I mean, Moses—is Whitney's ancestor and he's Monica's ancestor and he's Amber's and Fern's, that means . . ."

The Knitting Lady was nodding her head in encouragement. "Go ahead, Cal. Work through the logic."

"It means that Whitney, Monica, Fern, and Amber are all related. And me, too, only of course, I'm not."

"Like cousins?" Whitney asked. "We're all cousins?" Then she pointed to Fern and said, "I'm not related to *her*."

"You wish," Monica said back.

"When you wish upon a star . . . ," Fern started singing.

"See!" Whitney said. "See what I mean?"

The Knitting Lady scratched her head. "What I see is that I'm failing to make my point here. You're all resisting the connection. Why am I not g-getting through?"

Nobody had the answer for her, of course. I wanted to understand. I really did. But I couldn't believe that I was related to them. Any of them. Betty was my family.

Whitney didn't buy it either. "Jeez-Louise, just tell the story."

At that, the Knitting Lady froze. Her teeth were giving her bottom lip a good hard chew, so you could tell she was getting ready to say something important. If it had been me, I would have given Whitney a much-needed lecture about rudeness. But instead, the Knitting Lady's features softened. "You're right. It's best to just tell the story."

"A new one," Whitney demanded. "Something we haven't heard before."

"There is one sp-special story. But I don't think you're ready for it."

"Man-oh-man, that's what you always say about this story! We're ready for it!"

"It's c-complicated with lots of ancestors to keep track of."

Monica made a moaning sound. "I don't think I can follow it. I'm not good at complicated things."

"Me neither," Fern said. "But I'll try. I'll help you, Monica."

"If she tells it, you can't start laughing at everything," Whitney ordered.

Fern crossed her heart.

Meanwhile, the Knitting Lady's eyes were narrowing like two hands trying to hold on to something. I knew how *that* was—wanting to do something and not knowing if it's the right thing to do.

"Is it about a girl or a boy?" I asked.

The eyes let go. "Okay, you get your story. Take from it what you will."

"How does it start?" I asked.

The Knitting Lady closed her eyes and tilted her head up to the ceiling, like the story was written on the inside of her lids. All the tension around her face was gone. And when she opened her mouth, her voice was smooth and easy, no stutter at all, like she was singing us a song that began "The story of a girl who began to remember.

CHAPTER 10

"This is the story of a girl who began to remember. You don't need to hop on a magic carpet like in many stories you hear. The real distance is time."

"So this *is* a fairy tale!" Whitney said.

"No," Monica said. "It didn't start 'Once upon a time,' so it's true."

"True or not true, you have to start by imagining an old-fashioned, countrified past. There were acres of soil, rich and black enough to make you shiver. There were plum trees, an orchardful that had to be picked in late summer or else the fruit fell and rotted on the ground. What a stink! One by one, the plums were handpicked and then set out to bake in the sun. At first, it looked like chickens had laid little purple eggs in long, neat rows. But after a while, the fruit shriveled and turned into prunes."

"Ewww! I hate prunes," Monica said. "It means you're constipated, and I hate being constipated."

Whitney waved her off. "Forget about prunes! Go on with the story."

"The opening scene takes place in a building, a long,

no-nonsense rectangle, three floors high with more windows than you can count. Anyone could see that this was a building not to be questioned. It was painted such a gleaming white, it looked like it could deflect anything, even the impurities of the world."

Fern was all dreamy-eyed. "It sounds like a castle. I love a story with a castle."

"But a true story can't have a castle in it," Whitney complained.

"As a matter of fact," I said, "real castles exist, not only those in fairy tales."

The Knitting Lady continued. "All I'll say right now is that it looked like a castle. Every time people saw it nestled against the parched brown foothills, it startled them. The citizens of the nearby town said it looked like a great, white throne set against a carpet of wheat. They wanted to imagine that it was filled with princesses, poor but noble, being groomed to take their rightful place in the world. But for the people living inside, there was nothing romantic about the place."

"What was it?" I asked.

"There are so many names, and they all mean the same thing. An asylum, an institution, a mission, the Society, the Orphanage. It was a group home."

"Like this one?" Whitney asked.

"Much, much larger. There were a hundred girls at any

one time. And things were more permanent back in those days. It wasn't like today when you go in and out of various foster homes, or back and forth between your own family and group homes. Once a girl came in, she usually stayed."

Monica asked the question I was going to ask: "Did it have a name?" And the Knitting Lady answered: "The full and complete name was the Home for Orphaned and Indigent Children. The girls living there called it the Home. Many of them even came to think of it as home, even though most people in the world—if you could ask them— would say that a real home doesn't have a capital *H* and *the* in front of it. And now for the main character."

"A she!" Fern said, then turned to Whitney to brag. "See, I told you I could pay attention."

"The m-main character. Yes, a girl. The girl who began to remember. Like anyone who begins to remember, she first has things to forget. She was young when this story starts—about seven—and many things for the young are like a half-forgotten dream."

"She needs to have a name," Whitney insisted. "And don't just say *the girl*. You've pulled that one too much!"

"I agree. I call her Brenda. If you look up that name in a baby book, it means 'Little Raven.' Can you picture her? Her hair was raven black, so dark it had purple streaks. And shiny! A beautiful child. Her mother wasn't beautiful. She was glamorous, but only her hands—"

Fern interrupted. "Brenda's hands?"

"No, her mother's hands. They were something to behold, as wide as they were long and knotted with muscle."

Fern was still confused. "Knotted Hands is . . . ?"

Monica answered, "Brenda," but Whitney said, "No! The other one!"

The Knitted Lady made two fists and tapped one on top of the other. "Ahhh, I can see that I'm making this story way too confusing too soon. Let's go back to where Brenda's story begins. She's seven years old and she remembers arms lifting her from a bed and putting her into a car. She remembers a long drive in the middle of the night. She falls in and out of consciousness to the drone of the motor and the rhythm of voices from the front seat of the car. Her mother—"

"The glamorous one," I reminded everyone.

"Yes, that's her. Her mother muttered, 'Save me from one more town that ends in *ville.*'"

"In *ville,*" Fern mimicked, and started to laugh, but Whitney told her to zip it. "Go on," she urged the Knitting Lady.

"The man behind the wheel, who had a head of thick chestnut-colored hair, lit a cigarette, then blew smoke out the window. There were other memories attached to this particular day. Brenda's first sight of the Home off in the distance. The sound of her mother's voice, both wary and too enthusiastic: 'Look how white the building is. I'll say that for it. At least we know it's clean.' The man's wordless grunt. The long drive into the hills.

"When the car finally stopped, the man lifted Brenda, still dazed with sleepiness, out of the back seat. Her nose pressed against his jacket, the scent of tobacco mixing with the thick perfume of flowering plum trees in the morning air. An unfamiliar voice pulled Brenda out of her sleepy haze. A short, plain-faced woman, hands in the pockets of her apron, was looking at her and said, 'She does walk, doesn't she? We don't have no amenities here for a lame girl.'

"And then, her mother's voice again, 'She walks.'

"Without warning, Brenda's feet hit the ground, and she felt the man's hand in the small of her back, pushing her forward. 'Show the lady,' he ordered. 'Walk.'

"Brenda made a few hesitant marching steps, looking at her mother for approval. In return, Brenda got a weak smile. *This is not right,* she thought, and felt an uncomfortable twinge running through her, like when you drink something too cold and it goes right to your forehead. She looked around in a panic. There were girls everywhere, dozens of girls, some still in diapers, some already looking like adults, all dressed alike in white blouses and gray jumpers. Girls leaned on brooms, girls propped themselves on rakes, staring at her.

"Then Brenda's mother was down on one knee in front of her daughter. 'My darling girl, maybe a farm life will do you some good.' And then the man with the handsome head of hair took Brenda's mother by the arm, urging her back to her feet.

"'One minute,' she said to him, then turned back to Brenda. 'To remember me by.' She pressed something into Brenda's hand."

"What was it?" Monica asked.

"An unusual and very fancy pair of eyeglasses with a French name. Lorgnette. These glasses didn't hook around your ears, but had a gold handle to hold them up by. They were all the rage of glamorous ladies."

"What did Brenda say back?" I asked.

"Nothing. All she could do was watch her mother walk away."

"It was a big mistake," I said. "Her mother will come back."

"What m-makes you think that?"

"Because she will! It was a big mistake."

"N-no, Cal, it wasn't fair. But it wasn't a mistake."

"And then?" Whitney asked.

"And then— Girls, I'm sorry to say, we need to stop here."

"No! Don't stop!" Whitney begged.

"That's it?" Fern asked. "The end of the story? Did I miss something?"

"Come on," Monica whined. "I won't be able to sleep tonight. I'll be up *all* night worrying."

"Me too," Whitney said. "I have a thousand questions!"

Still, the Knitting Lady couldn't be persuaded to continue. It was my first sign of just how stubborn she could be. She pushed herself to standing. "Brenda's story has w-way too many twists and turns for one sitting. But don't worry. We'll get to them all. Brenda isn't going anywhere for a long time."

Fern's arm shot up. She waved it around. "One question. Please, just one? Please, it's important." The Knitting Lady held up one finger, and we all waited to see which of the thousand questions would be answered.

"So my question is," Fern said, "are we having prunes for dinner or not?"

CHAPTER 11

Later that afternoon, we all went to a park. It was only a few blocks away, but by the time we got there, we were dragging from the heat. The Knitting Lady had a conversation with a Parks and Rec type of person who turned on the sprinklers and let us run through them. Monica and Fern held hands and squealed, glowing like this was the best day of their lives. Amber looked happy, too. It was the first time I had actually seen her smile. She had the straightest whitest teeth. Whitney, soaking wet, took a flying leap and flung herself belly first on a swing.

After running through the sprinkler, I shook myself off like a dog and found a tree to sit under. Whitney motioned for me to join her on the swings, but I waved her off. That's another way I'm like Betty. I can stand being around people only for so long without needing to get off by myself. How else can a person think?

And I had things to think about, such as those fancy French glasses that had been placed in Brenda's hands. The look of them. The feel of them. Brenda's situation was certainly bad, but at least she had her mother's fancy glasses. What did I have of Betty's? Nothing! Not even a piece of hair, not a scarf with her smell, not a scrap of paper with her tight handwriting that always reminded me of barbed wire. This thought turned around and around in my head until I realized with a sick feeling that I had no proof that my mother was my mother, that she ever even existed.

I shivered, and it had nothing to do with being wet.

Stop! Stop! Stop! I, Cal Lavender, refused to give in to thoughts like that. I would just have to keep myself busy until Betty came for me. Put *that* in the story of my real life: *Cal Lavender knows the secret of avoiding certain thoughts. She keeps busy.*

By the time we got back to the Pumpkin House, I had the perfect "keeping busy" project in mind. My temporary roommates definitely needed some serious help in the room-cleaning-and-organization department. Most typical, average eleven-year-old girls would rather clip their toenails with a chain saw than clean their rooms, but organization is something that I really excel at. It was practically a requirement for living with Betty. If I didn't have an orderly system for just about everything, meals would never be made, my homework would wind up in the trash, we would have to wear dirty underwear, and, as I mentioned before, that's no way to walk around. To my way of thinking, organization is a beautiful and necessary thing.

That's exactly what I said to Whitney and Amber. I stood in the middle of the messy bedroom and said, "Organization is a beautiful and necessary thing. What on earth is *this* doing here?"

Whitney was on her bed reading a comic book. "What's *what* doing *where*?"

I held up a toothbrush. "This." Then I hooked my finger into the back of one of her shoes and let it dangle. "This doing in here."

"That's where I keep it," she said.

"Why?"

"Because then I know exactly where my toothbrush is."

I thought: *This is going to be a long road. It will take me several days to just make a dent in this mess, but I'm not going to be here that long. Still, I'll do what I can. This will be my legacy to them. Years from now, Whitney and Amber will recall fondly: Remember that girl who was here for only a day or two? That Cal Lavender really taught us a thing or two about the beauty of organization.*

"I'm going to clean," I said. "Yes, that's what I'm going to do." I began my attack by giving the toothbrush a proper home in the bathroom down the hall. Then I picked up the pile of Whitney's clothes that were all over the floor like roadkill. I folded each piece and you couldn't find better folding in the finest department stores.

But where was I supposed to put all the perfectly

folded laundry? Whitney's drawers were already overflowing. And what should I do with her shoes? The closet, I guess. I opened the door. They joined about a million other things stuffed in there. From the floor, I started picking up candy wrappers, gum wrappers, toothpicks, and about two dozen cellophane sleeves, the kind that keeps string cheese in fresh and sanitary individual portions. I moved Ike Eisenhower the Fifth from the messy dresser top to a messy desktop. Then I picked up what I thought were pieces of broken greenish plastic, but they turned out to be old, moldy, unsanitary pieces of string cheese.

By this point, I was hoping that my temporary roommates would catch some of my cleaning fever and join in enthusiastically. I sighed. I gave a bigger sigh. I sighed again. I know they heard me, but they went deaf all of a sudden. Amber sat watching me like I was a stage show, *The Sound of Scrubbing.* It was creepy. But to my mind, being creepy is absolutely no excuse for being a slob.

I asked, "Can she talk?"

Whitney looked up. "Huh?"

"Can Amber talk?"

"Can a . . . can a *what* poop in the woods?"

"A bear," I answered.

"Yeah, a bear can poop in the woods, and Amber can talk. Can't you, Amber?"

Amber nodded, which was infuriating because, if she

could talk, that was the time to do it. Whitney kept eating her sunflower seeds—*crack, crack*—which covered the carpet, like she expected April showers to come in and turn them into May flowers.

I said, "Whitney, are you afraid of getting lost in here?"

She looked up from the comic book. "Huh?"

I paused for effect. "Like Hansel and Gretel? Are you leaving a trail of seeds so that you can find your way back to your bed?"

Whitney started humming "Whistle While You Work." When she got to the chorus, she stopped and said, "My fifth foster mother was like you. A real cleaning nut. Once a week, she made us do 'Cleaning Madness.' It took hours and wrecked a perfectly good Saturday afternoon. My job was to rake the wall-to-wall carpet. Man-oh-man, all the nap had to go in the same direction."

Personally, I did not see what was so outrageous about that. I bet it looked a whole lot nicer than wall-to-wall shells. "Well, no offense, but anyone would be a cleaning nut compared to you. Face it, Whitney. You're organizationally challenged!" I turned to Amber and said, "You, too."

Whitney laughed like *How amusing,* crossed her legs, and pretended to be smoking a cigarette in a glamorous way. "You may clean the toilet next."

"Well, it *does* need it," I said.

"Go wild," she said.

Some people would have stopped cleaning on the spot and let Whitney and Amber roll around in their own mess. But when Cal Lavender gets mad, she gets cleaning. Come to think of it, when I get sad, I also clean. I really throw myself into it until I get lost in all the moving and dusting and organizing and scrubbing. It's my way of forgetting about everything else.

I ricocheted around the room, squirting Endust and wiping down every surface. Door frames, door handles, table legs, baseboards. I must have taken an inch layer of dust off the windowsill alone. An *inch*! I wiped the outside of Ike Eisenhower the Fifth's home. I emptied the overflowing trashcan. I was about to tackle the black hole of a closet when Whitney called me back from the Land of Spic-and-Span by saying, "Whatever you do, don't look in there."

"In where?" I asked. "The closet?"

"No, there." She pointed across the room at her dresser.

"I'm not anywhere near your dresser."

"Good. Whatever you do, don't look in there. Especially the bottom drawer."

I tried to ignore her, but it was no use. Most people are like that, right? You tell them not to think about pink elephants, and all they can do then is think about pink elephants. "Why shouldn't I look in there?" I took two steps closer.

Whitney glanced around the room suspiciously like she was certain that foreign agents, the CIA, the county school board, and the anchorman on the nightly news were all eavesdropping. "It's the PICTURE," she said. That's the way she said it, like the word *picture* was in capital letters or in special print.

"What picture?"

"Amber has seen the PICTURE. Right, Amber?"

Amber nodded.

Whitney's hand went to her mouth. *Crack-crack.* Her eyes narrowed into slits. *Crack-crack.* "You wanna see it?"

"Sure," I said.

"Say *really, really.*"

"Really, really."

"Okay then." She hopped out of bed, opened the drawer, dug to the very bottom, and handed something flat to me. "Don't bend it!" she ordered.

It was a photograph of a little girl and was already bent, crumpled too, like she had pulled it in and out of the drawer three times a day for the past five years. The girl in the picture was about three. Her back was to the camera, but she was peeking over her shoulder so that you could see part of her face. She also happened to be buck naked in that cute, Jell-O–bottom, three-year-old way.

I looked up for an explanation. Whitney was beaming. "That's her."

"Her?"

"Tell her, Amber. That's my sister. Right, Amber?"

The Amber nod again.

I looked closer at the photo. "I thought you said you don't have any family."

"I *said* I don't have any parents. I have a sister. She got adopted because she didn't have a hole in her heart. Now she's looking for me. Tell her, Amber."

Amber's eyes went wide, and for a moment, I actually thought she was going to speak. But even if she had wanted to, there was no breaking in on Whitney, who was really on a roll: "Amber had a dream about her. A dream! That's a sign, all right. She's the older sister, two years older. But she needs me. I have to go to her."

I asked, "Where does she live?"

Again that Whitney look of disgust that told me I did not know much about anything worth knowing. "How would I know where she lives? When someone gets adopted, they don't tell you anything about where they went. Sometimes, the new parents even change the kid's name just because they feel like it."

"So how are you going to track her down?"

Whitney waved the picture like she was drying it. "I'll recognize her, of course."

"By that?" I asked in disbelief. "It's all out of focus. Besides, she won't look like this anymore."

"Look here!" Whitney was stabbing the end of her fingernail at the photo.

I looked over her shoulder. "What am I supposed to be looking at?"

"The birthmark! My sister has a little veiny thing, a bump, right on her left butt cheek. It's shaped like a heart."

I was looking hard. I was really trying to see something, but there was nothing to see. I pressed my tongue against my front teeth and ran Whitney's plan—if you could call it a plan—through my mind: *Let me see if I have this right. The last time Whitney saw her sister, the girl was running around in diapers, only without the diaper. She doesn't know her sister's name. She doesn't know where she lives. The only thing she has to go on is an old photo and a birthmark that hardly exists. Wrong, wrong, wrong.*

There was something definitely not normal about Whitney's logic. I said in a very polite way, "Excuse me, Whitney, but are you intending to walk up to every twelve-year-old girl in the world and ask to see her bottom?"

Whitney: *Crack-crack.*

I continued politely and logically. "Frankly, your plan has problems."

Whitney: Louder, faster *crack-crack-crack*. She stopped cracking. "It does not."

"I have to be honest," I said. "It's totally illogical. Frankly, it's a touch not normal. Truthfully, it's insane."

Whitney ripped the picture away from my eyes. "Well, you should know plenty about insane."

I asked cautiously, "What do you mean by that?"

"I snuck a peek at your social-worker file and your mother is plenty insane. She insaned all over the library!"

I said nothing.

"Crazy," she said. "C-R-A-Z-I-E."

Whitney's words were making me feel like I had just fallen off a jungle gym and landed so hard on my back that all my breathing caught high in my chest. What did Whitney know about Betty? What did she know about anything?

She turned to Amber. "Betty's in the funny farm. What do people *do* in the funny farm anyway? They must plant seeds and water the clowns that grow. Get it? The *funny* farm."

Whitney kept saying "funny farm, funny farm," and I had my hands clamped over my ears, ordering myself to ignore her. I called on my special power, not a superpower or anything like that, but a strength that I taught myself to conjure up whenever I need it. *You will not cry. You will not cry!!*

I WILL NOT CRY! And when I was absolutely, one hundred percent sure that I wouldn't, I looked Whitney right in the face and said, "At least I have a mother."

That stopped her. That shut her up! She winced like someone getting a scraped knee cleaned with alcohol. Then her eyes began widening, wider and wider like she was trying to inhale me through them. She reached out and pressed her hand over my mouth like a gas mask. I slapped it away. She started to say, "Library," so I yelled, "Mother!"

Through the walls, I could hear Monica and Fern yelling, "Fight! Fight!" I turned to Amber—"What are you looking at?"—and took giant steps out of the room.

On my way down the stairs, I vowed: *Nobody will ever know what happened in the library!*

CHAPTER 12

Here's what happened in the library:

From what I can tell, average grown-ups have trained themselves not to think about all the stupid, scary, and hurtful things in the world. If they thought too much about them, they couldn't get out of bed in the morning. And if they couldn't get out of bed in the morning, who would take care of the cooking, cleaning, teaching, shopping, taxpaying, and all that other adult business? Who would drive the buses?

But anyone who knows Betty knows that she is not an average grown-up. She's more like a kid. Things get to her. Usually I could sense when trouble was starting to build up inside. She'd sleep too much, then stop sleeping altogether. She'd talk and talk, but then suddenly I wouldn't be able to get a word out of her. Mostly though, it showed in her eyes, the way they'd be burning way too bright, like supernovas, two distant unreachable stars that are ready to explode.

That day at the library, I must have fallen asleep. Because the next thing I remember was seeing volume F of the *World Book Encyclopedia* flying through the air. Then, *The Complete Guide to Learning and Loving Ballet* hit the floor across the room. All over the reading room, heads lifted from their necks and swiveled in our direction like they were controlled by machinery. Betty threw more books, and arms went up in defense.

I remember an alarm ringing. Shouts. Screams. People running. Elbows pushing this way and that. I remember ordering myself, *Do something! Do something!*

And then all went silent for a second as Betty sat back down at our table and plopped forward at the waist. Her arms were spread, and her face lay flat against the table. She looked like a puppet whose strings had been cut. I heard someone say, "Don't put the child at risk."

The child. That was me. I wanted to say: *I'm not at risk. Just leave us alone. Let me take care of things. I always know what to do.* But I didn't say anything.

Why didn't I say anything? In the Knitting Lady's story, Brenda didn't say anything either. Why?

And then another voice in the library said, "I'm going to try to get closer. She's calm now."

But I knew better. They should have asked me. I knew that Betty was only on hold. Her eyes opened—*thwock!*—like parachutes. A wail went up and then her wails filled the room, like she was drawing sadness from every sad story in every sad book in the library.

Why didn't I notice her eyes earlier? Why didn't I see the signs? If I had only looked closer. If only I hadn't fallen asleep.

So that's what happened in the library. But nobody in the Pumpkin House will ever know. They would never understand. Nothing like that ever happened to them. Ever!

CHAPTER 13

"I am *not* staying in that bedroom."

I found the Knitting Lady alone in Talk Central. Her hands were a whirl of yarn and needles. "What's wrong with the b-bedroom? You have the nicest room, in my opinion. But don't tell Fern and Monica I said that."

"It's not the bedroom. Something's wrong with Whitney. Amber, too. I'm sure you've noticed." I tapped my index finger to my temple and made little cuckoo circles. "The polite term for them is head cases."

"P-polite? I'd hate to hear the— Dang!" She held up the long rectangle she was knitting. There was a puzzled look on her face.

"Did you mess up?" I asked.

She shushed me. "Give me a sec." She began counting the number of loops on her needle. "One, two . . ." At seventy-one, she said "Dang!" again. "I knew it. I dropped a stitch somewhere. Help me find it."

I knew zilch about knitting, but finding things was my specialty. Betty was always losing something, and it was always up to me to find it. But where should I look? When you drop a stitch, how far can it go? Does it bounce or roll? I don't like admitting that I don't know something, so I started checking in the most logical place, under the couch.

Above me, I heard the Knitting Lady laugh. "It doesn't take off *that* far."

She held up her knitting to study it. I looked closely at the shades of purple, but I didn't see anything that looked like a dropped stitch. Not that I knew what a dropped stitch looked like, but I expected to see something cracked or hanging off at least.

"Nothing," I said.

"I don't see it either. But I know it's h-here somewhere."

"How do you know you dropped it if you don't see it?"

"I've been at this long enough to feel it in my bones. My rhythm felt off. So I counted, and sure enough one is missing."

"Can you fix it?"

"S-sure. Everything can be fixed. I go backward and find the source of the mistake."

She slipped the needle out of her work and started unraveling. My stomach winced as I watched all those nice, even rows disappearing. That's another thing you can say about me: *Cal Lavender is a stomach person, the way some people are headache people or ache-in-the-back people.* The stomach is where I feel things first.

I asked, "How long did it take you to knit all that?"

"This? A couple of hours. This y-yarn isn't the easiest to work with. And the needles are small. It's a new pattern for me, and a hard one at that. But the hardest ones are the most rewarding when you finally get it right."

She handed me the balls of yarn and showed me how to wind the unraveled strands onto their matching color.

"Doesn't this make you frustrated?" I asked.

"Of c-course. I'm like everyone else. I like things to run nice and smooth. When I first started knitting, I was younger than you and used to get furious when I had to rip out my work. Furious! But mistakes are inevitable. Especially when you're working with something new, before you get in sync with it."

"What if you ignored the mistake? Does one . . . what did you call it?"

"A dr-dropped stitch."

"One of those doesn't sound like the end of the world. You have so many others. What does one matter?"

"B-believe you me, you're not the first to come up with that bright idea. It seems logical enough, and I have personally tried ignoring my mistakes, only to find myself in a real knitting pickle later on. One little mistake influences every stitch that comes after it. Trust me, in the long run it's best to go back and clear it up. There's no way around it."

I repeated after her, "Clear it up?"

"Start fresh," she said. "Sometimes you just get off on the wrong f-foot. You're a smart girl. You see what I'm getting at."

I didn't. Not until just that moment anyway. Then I recognized the tone that grown-ups get when they're trying to slip in some advice or a really big life lesson. As I rewound the conversation in my head, all the telltale words were there.

Ignoring mistakes. Going back to the beginning. Getting in sync. Starting fresh.

"Are you talking about knitting? Or something else?"

She didn't miss a beat. "What else do you have in mind? What else do you think I might be talking about?"

But before I had a chance to answer, she shouted, "Got it!"

"Got what?"

"The dropped stitch. See, it wasn't very far back. Now it's no problem at all to correct. I join it to the others. Then I can move forward again."

I knew what she was trying to say. It was one of those life lessons, all right. Whitney and Amber and I had gotten off on the wrong foot, and I should go back and correct my mistake so that I don't find myself in a pickle down the line.

"I know what you're saying, but I still want to change my room," I insisted.

"*Ahhhh,*" she said. "If you're going to bitch, then you might as well stitch."

It was funny hearing something like that coming out of her mouth. *Stitch* and *bitch*. That sounded more like something Betty would come up with, which made me wonder what my mother would think of the Knitting Lady and vice versa. They definitely weren't anything like each other. They were more like exact opposites. Betty was . . . well, Betty. And the Knitting Lady had a way of being calm that made you think that everything is running smoothly, that there really aren't any problems in the world, at least no problems that can't somehow be fixed.

But still, they would hit it off. I just knew they would. Betty would tell the Knitting Lady her stories. The Knitting Lady wouldn't rub her temples as if it gave her a headache just to be around Betty. They would like each other. They would.

"Your turn," the Knitting Lady said, and handed me a pair of knitting needles. They were different than hers. These were as long and thick as drumsticks. "Ready for a good old-fashioned stitch-and-bitch?"

CHAPTER 14

Knitting lesson number one: A dropped stitch is only the beginning of all the possible mistakes a person can make. You can add a stitch. You can twist a stitch. You can purl when you are supposed to knit and knit when you are supposed to purl. A purl, by the way, is a backward knit stitch, which is sometimes exactly what you want. But when you don't do it on purpose, a purl is an ugly screwup that sticks out like a pimple on your nose.

The Knitting Lady began by teaching me the basic knit stitch, which was easy enough, especially when she put the rhyme to it. She said, "In through the front door / run around the back / peek through the window / off jumps Jack."

Translation: You stick the needle into the first loop, wrap the yarn around it, then pull it through, up and off the top.

Normally I'm not the braggy type, but I was a total and complete natural at knitting. I'm sure the Knitting Lady had never seen anyone take to it like I did. I made one stitch, then another. Pretty soon, my hands were flying and I found myself at the end of the row. Then with just about no help at all, I flipped the needles around and started back down the other side.

Only, by the time I got to the seventh row, things were not going quite so smoothly. I couldn't get in the front door. In frustration, I jammed a needle through the loop. There, that worked. Only the loop looked all mangled. Plus it had a death grip around both needles.

I was deep in a knitting pickle.

"Got a problem with Jack?" the Knitting Lady asked. She took my knitting and examined it. "Ahhhh, the tight-stitch type."

"What's that mean?" I asked.

"Everyone has a t-tendency. I could tell from the minute I looked at you. I said to myself, *Cal Lavender is the tight-stitch type.* I'm a stitch reader."

"Like a palm reader?"

"Sort of. Only I don't care so much about the future. The present is much more interesting, and that's what your stitches reveal. They tell me all about who you are right n-now, at this very moment."

She picked up a tangle of yarn and needles that were bunched up on the floor by her feet. What a mess! It was the wildest looking thing, oranges and purples with a whole lot of loose ends snaking out. Somebody had no taste in colors at all!

"Take this, for instance. A loose-stitch type. Definitely,"

she said. "I look at this, and I see someone whose personality is all loosey-goosey, the opposite of yours."

It didn't take a genius to know who did it. "Whitney," I said. "It's an obvious mess. It is so . . ."

"*So* Whitney, isn't it? Who else would put these wacky colors together? It's so much fun, it makes me laugh."

Personally, I didn't see what kind of fun she saw in it. It made me laugh—*Ha!*—but not in the nice way the Knitting Lady meant. "Tight definitely has it over being loosey-goosey," I decided. "A million to one."

"One's not better than the other. They can both be strengths. But they can both also be w-weaknesses. Whitney's knitting has trouble holding together. But it's so full of surprises. Sort of like Whitney."

"What does Monica's knitting reveal?"

"W-what do you think?"

"My guess is that she won't even try. She would say that she can't do it, that she doesn't know how, even before she tried."

"I-I'm working on her!" the Knitting Lady said cheerfully.

"And Fern? Hmmm. I bet she starts something and can't remember where she put it and then starts something else new. Am I right?"

The Knitting Lady nodded with encouragement. "Hey, you have the stitch-reading power in you, too."

I held up my knitting. "So what does mine say?"

She put her hand to her temple and did a corny swirling motion like she was going into a trance. "I see precision, a love of order. I see a girl who likes to do things perfectly and often succeeds at it."

Definitely right! "So what's the weakness?"

She patted my knitting like it was her favorite pet, then handed it back. "You tell me. You're the one w-working with it."

It *was* precise. It *was* perfect. It was really something! Except . . . "I guess if I don't loosen up a little, I'll be stuck in the same place forever. How do I loosen up?"

She pulled the needle off the tight stitches. I thought I heard them sigh in relief. "You loosen up your knitting by loosening up yourself. You feel the looseness starting here." She tapped the crown of my head. "Let the looseness travel down through your neck into your hands and out your fingers. Think loose. No! Don't *think* loose. *Be* loose."

I unraveled. "Loose," I said aloud. Then in my head: *Loose, loose.*

I was back to the beginning. This time I was sure I would get it right. I will be loose. I WILL be loose. I WILL BE LOOSE! Only by the time I got to row five, the stitches were strangling the needle again. I didn't even get as far as the last time. How did this happen? Why couldn't I do it right? When the Knitting Lady examined my work, all I wanted to do was apologize.

"For what?" she asked. "For not immediately getting it right? For not being p-perfect? You'll get it. It takes time. Let me ask you an important question: What's the first thing you need when you start a piece of knitting?"

What kind of riddle was this? I tried, "Needles?"

She shook her head no. "Try again."

"Yarn?"

"Nope. Whitney, you want to tell her?"

I had been so engrossed in staying *loose, loose* that I didn't notice Whitney standing at the door. I looked up, then quickly away.

"Uh? Tell her what?" she asked.

"What is the f-first thing you need when you start knitting?"

Whitney answered quickly: "Peace of mind."

CHAPTER 15

Whitney plopped on a chair. She gave me a *glad to see you, glad to see your face* look, which took me by surprise. She didn't look mad or embarrassed or like her stomach hurt, any of the things that a logical person feels right after she's made a brand-new enemy for life. I put on My Face for Unbearably Unpleasant and Embarrassing Situations to show her that I would never fall for phony friendliness. But that was a waste of time, since she didn't even notice. She was too busy bobbing up and down in front of the Knitting Lady, blurting things out. "Come on, come on! It's time. We've waited. Can we? Can you? Come on! Pleeeeease. You promised. Where were we?"

I don't know how the Knitting Lady had the slightest clue what Whitney was talking about, but she answered, "Brenda."

"Get on with it," Whitney ordered.

"Okay. But first, g-gather everyone together."

⌇

"Do you r-remember where I stopped? Brenda has arrived at the Home. More than anything, she wanted her life to remain the way it had always been. Now, some people might have trouble understanding that. They would have looked at Brenda's life and thought that it was no life at all for a child. Her mother had dragged Brenda from one town to another and had never given her a permanent home. Many people would have been shocked by the number of boyfriends who had passed through her mother's life. *Shocked!* But Brenda didn't remember any of that. A child remembers what she needs to. This was what Brenda called life, and now she felt everything familiar slipping away.

"Her mother got into the car and said something to the man next to her. He started the engine. The car turned around and headed down the long driveway. The whole time Brenda just stood there gazing out into the distance and waiting for the car to make a U-turn and fly back, tires squealing. But when the car disappeared into a tiny dot on the horizon—*Oh!*—she was outraged. Anger rose from her pores like a gas. A voice screamed. A hand hurled those fancy French glasses to the ground. Brenda barely recognized the voice and the hand. They were hers, of course, but she was too furious to stop herself."

"I like Brenda," Whitney said. "She didn't just stand there and take it."

"Go on," Monica encouraged. "What happened next?"

"I s-suppose I could do that. I could move on from there and tell the story in a nice straightforward, logical manner. But that won't do. It would make it seem like Brenda was just the beginning and the end of her own separate line. What nonsense! So let's leave Brenda now."

"No!" Whitney shouted.

"D-don't worry. Her story isn't going anywhere. There are too many connections. Everything that happened in the past leads to it; the future backs right up to it. We have to go back to the story of Brenda's mother. Let's call her Lillian."

"She's the glamorous one, right?" Fern asked.

"Exactly! G-good for you for remembering. Now, all of you, close your eyes and go back even further in time. There was no TV yet. People had to leave their homes to get entertainment. Now picture a butcher shop on the main street of a small town. In the window, there is a thick cardboard placard."

J. S. BERRY'S DRAMA-VARIETY THEATER, ### *the Grand Inaugural of the Summer Season*.

FEATURING **ARCHEY HUGHES**, *an Old-Timey Singer*.
TOMMY GRANGER—*Bringing a Lifelike Imitation of a Jockey after a Ride*.
SWAIN'S BIRDS—*a Bevy of Feathered Thespians*.

I started laughing. I couldn't help it. Whitney was doubled over. Amber had a small grin, which was a major show of emotion for her. Monica was cracking up. Fern was really out of control—Ha! Ha! Ha! Ha! Ha! Ha! Ha! Ha! Ha! Even when the rest of us stopped laughing, she was still going Ha! Ha! Ha! Ha! Ha! Ha!—until she finally caught her breath and asked the Knitting Lady, "So *what* are we laughing at again?"

"V-vaudeville! You girls have to understand that there were posters like that all across the country, in every small town. That's what entertainment was in those days. Nothing today—not even a circus—comes close to the amazing events you could see for only twenty-five cents! On this same bill there was also *Lovely Lillian with Her Delightfully Dexterous Digits!!!!!!!!!!* Ten exclamation points after her title! One for each digit! She must have been something!"

"Digits?" Whitney asked

"Fingers," I explained. "Or toes."

Monica was shaking her head. "What kind of entertainment is digits?"

"We'll g-get to that. But first, we need to go back even further to before Lillian became the *Lovely Lillian.* Her story opens when she was a young girl in New York City. This was a long time ago, around the turn of the previous century. Back then, it was always hard times, never a break. A lot of people couldn't even manage to squeak by. Groups of kids ran wild all day and all night. Lillian lived in a small, noisy apartment with her mother and—"

"No father?" Monica asked.

"No father. Lillian's father left before she was born. It had always been just her and her mother. On a shelf in their tiny apartment sat a pair of fancy spectacles. They were gold—real gold—thin and light as wire."

"The . . . the . . . you know . . . the whatchamacallits!" Fern called out.

I translated for everyone in a very proper French accent, "The word is *lorgnette.*"

"Exactly. K-keep in mind that Lillian and her mother were so poor that they owned nothing that didn't serve some practical use. Except for the lorgnette. These stood in such sharp contrast to their pitiful surroundings that Lillian couldn't keep her eyes off them.

"Lillian's mother was very young and different from a lot of the other adults in this run-down neighborhood. For one thing, she knew how to read and write. And what a lovely voice came out of her mother's mouth. That was their bread and butter. Each morning, Lillian and her mother trudged off to the docks. All day, they stood singing and begging for coins."

"Lillian had a lovely voice, too?" I asked.

"To put it bluntly, n-no. The poor child could not carry a tune, couldn't dance either. When it came to performing, truthfully, our Lillian was pathetic."

"How embarrassing!" Monica said. "I would die of embarrassment."

"B-but not Lillian. She was quite an individual. Most children normally shy away from what they can't do well. But a complete and total lack of talent didn't stop Lillian. Not for a minute! She was a plain little thing, but she already knew that she liked being looked at. Really liked it! On the street corners, she caterwauled and stomped and stumbled over her own feet. She was unstoppable."

"Like this?" Whitney stood and shuffled her feet.

Fern jumped up, too, and moved so fast that her feet slipped out in front of her and she fell to the floor, laughing of course.

"That's exactly the style. Whitney, Fern, you both definitely have some Lillian in you! Even though Lillian was wearing rags, she presented herself to the world as if she were dressed in silk and crinolines. Then one day, everything changed."

"Oh, no!" Monica said.

"Oh, no, what?" Fern asked. "What?"

The Knitting Lady paused. She put down her yarn and needles and looked at us in a serious way. I felt that she was most especially looking at me. "It can happen that way, can't it? One day, things are one way. And the next day, the life you are living, what you call life, changes forever."

CHAPTER 16

"Not forever!" I insisted.

"In this case, yes, forever." The Knitting Lady shook her head. "It's sad. Very, very sad."

Monica took a pillow from the couch and hugged it to her middle. "This is going to be scary. I'm going to have nightmares about this. I know I will."

"Sad?" Fern asked. She scanned faces frantically. "What did I miss? Who's sad? Who's having nightmares?"

Something hard and heavy dropped to the pit of my stomach. *Someone died. The last thing I want to hear is a story where someone dies because dead, dead, dead, that's all I'll think about. Betty and a coffin and that pie-crust makeup. Dead is dead is dead. Forever.*

Monica said what I was thinking, "I hope no one died. I hate a story where somebody dies."

"Not me," Whitney said. "It hardly counts as a story unless someone dies. Especially a mysterious, gruesome death. I saw a dead body once. It had maggots and everything coming out of its eyes."

Monica blanched. "Stop it. You never saw a dead person. You're saying that to scare me. Don't do that!"

Whitney crossed her heart. "Hope to die, it's the truth. Get it? Hope to *die*." Then, she addressed the Knitting Lady, "Did someone die or not?"

"Unfortunately, y-yes. There was a death. It was Lillian's mother. I think you all suspected that. I'm sorry, but that's what happened. One day she was singing and the next day she got a cough and the day after that, the cough got worse. Pneumonia."

"I had pneumonia once, in my sixth foster home," Whitney said. "But I didn't die. At least then, I didn't die. There was the other time when—"

I interrupted, "There's a time for silence, Whitney, and this is it." I pressed the Knitting Lady. "Go on."

"For L-Lillian, there were so many memories attached to this tragedy. For instance, her mother's casket and how it sat on top of a large tank of ice in their apartment."

"Gross!" Monica blurted out.

"That's h-how they did things in those days. Everyone in the apartment building came to pay their respects. Neighbors filtered in and out. The religious ones crossed themselves. Nobody knew the dead woman well, and, if the truth be told, none of them cared much for what little they knew. She had always seemed to be putting on airs, the way she carried herself in a straight-backed way like she was better than her surroundings. Still, a great many neighbors cried when they looked at the young mother on a block of ice."

"Did Lillian look at her mother?" I asked.

Monica covered her face: "No, I wouldn't look. Never, ever!"

"Wh-what do you think, Cal? Can you put yourself in Lillian's shoes?"

"I think she wanted to look," I began. "But then again, she wouldn't want to. Like when you know there's a really scary part in a movie and you try to keep your eyes open, but at the last second, you put your hands over them."

"It was a l-lot like that. Lillian would approach, then at the last second scurry off to a closet or dive under a table, her heart pounding. Then for hours, she sat on the floor in a corner of the room, knees drawn to her chest, silent. For probably the first time in her life, the girl wanted no attention at all. Still, neighbors kept urging her to say a final farewell to her mother. A woman with big teeth came right up to Lillian's eyes. 'Come on and be a big girl,' she insisted. 'Pay your respects. Say something.'

"But Lillian put on a face she invented herself, a hard, scowling face that drove the woman away. It wasn't that Lillian wasn't thinking about her mother. Of course, she was thinking about her. For days, she had been thinking of nothing else. But after a while, Lillian just didn't know what to think anymore. She had run out of thoughts, the way you can run out of tears. Everything was numb. So what could she say? What does a girl say when her mother has died? What words are there?"

Fern gave a nervous laugh.

"None," Monica said. "There are no words."

"So in her h-head, where no one could hear, Lillian conducted her own farewell ritual. She sang a song her mother was always singing. Then she sang another. We all have our own way of mourning and of saying good-bye to the people we love. This was Lillian's homage.

"At some point, without even realizing it herself, she began to sing her mother's favorite tunes aloud. She sang 'Take Me Out to the Ball Game.' And she sang 'In the Good Old Summertime.' How does that song go again? It was so popular way back when. *You hold her hand, and she holds yours, / and that's a very good sign. / That she's your tootsy-wootsy, / in the good old summertime.* Lillian got so caught up in her singing—her loud, off-key singing—that she didn't notice when two strangers, a woman and a man, walked into the apartment."

"Uh-oh," Whitney said. "Here comes trouble."

"How do you know that?" I asked.

"It's obvious. In stories, strangers are trouble." Whitney turned to the Knitting Lady. "Trouble, right? So they walked in and—"

"*Walked* is the wrong w-word for the way these two entered. They made an entrance. They floated. They seemed to take up all the space and air in the room even though there were only two of them. Once or twice, Lillian and her mother had ventured out of their neighborhood to gaze at the clothing in the windows of fancy shops on fancy streets. Fancy was how the woman dressed, all lace and silk and satin that made a swishing noise when she turned. The man wore a thick black cloak made of the finest wool and carried a broad-brimmed hat.

"As the man looked around the apartment, his eyebrows shot up in a judgmental arch. The woman's nose crinkled and twitched as though it was the first time in her life that she had ever smelled anything that wasn't fresh from the laundry. She cleared her throat: 'We hear there is a child. Is that the child over there?' "

Fern started singing: " 'She's your wootsy-tootsy. In the one, two, three strikes you're out time.' "

"Exactly!" the Knitting Lady said. "Lillian was still singing her heart out. The man in the black cloak got a distasteful expression on his face.

" 'Tsk, tsk,' he said. 'Singing at a tragic time like this!' And the woman in satin and lace responded, 'What do you expect? Look at how she was raised.' Then she pointed at one of the neighbors, a man from down the hall who had arms the size of hams. 'You! Yes, you. Bring the child here!' Before Lillian realized what was happening, a pair of thick, hairy arms lifted her and carried her across the room. Then she felt her feet hit the ground, her ankles buckling slightly.

"The rich woman studied her. 'Not at all delicate and

fair like Cousin. Must take after the father.' She made that last word—*father*—sound slick and oily. 'Still, she appears strong.'

"Then the strangers formed a tight twosome, their heads bowed, their shoulders touching. There was a lot of whispering, and Lillian heard many hard, hissing *S*s. 'Yes, yes, Reverend, I simply agree. She must say good-bye. After all, Cousin was her mother.'

"At that, the man, this well-dressed reverend, approached Lillian. His lower lip was pressed forward. He lifted her up and when she looked down, she saw her mother who wasn't her mother.

" 'Say good-bye, child,' the Reverend coaxed. 'She's at peace now.'

" 'Peace?' the rich woman said with scorn. 'After the pain she caused to her family? After she threw away everything for . . . this?'

"The woman's arm made a sweeping motion around the room, and then her face widened with surprise. She walked to the shelf and picked up the only thing of luxury and refined taste in the room."

"The lorgnette," I said.

"S-she ran her fingers over the engraving and held it up to her face. Lillian, still suspended in the air, nothing solid under her feet, was struck for the first time in her life by a great desire to escape."

CHAPTER 17

"So," Fern said. "I guess the mother died, huh?"

Whitney threw up her hands: "Is the pope . . . Is the pope . . . Is the pope what, Cal?"

"Catholic," I answered.

"Yeah, the pope is Catholic and the mother died!" Whitney snapped. Then she went on with a million questions: "Who are the rich people? What did Lillian's mother do wrong? Why is the pope Catholic? Can you sing the funny song again?"

The Knitting Lady pushed down the air with her palms. "Slow down, Whitney. Anyone want to take a stab at the first question? Who are the rich people?"

I was about to answer, "Lillian's relatives," when the Knitting Lady said, "That's right, Amber. You know."

My head snapped around. This was not a yes-or-no question that Amber could answer with a nod. She couldn't get away with that! Finally, the moment I had been waiting for. Would she or wouldn't she? Could she or couldn't she? Amber's lips began moving and something was coming out. Words. They were so soft that I had to strain to hear them. "The rich people are . . ."

The Knitting Lady encouraged her. "Go on, Amber. You've got it."

A little louder now, more secure. "They're Lillian's mother's la-de-dah relatives."

"La-de-dah?" Monica asked.

"She used to be rich, too."

Fern still didn't get it. "Who used to be rich?"

Whitney nudged me. "I don't get it either."

But I understood. I got it! And Amber understood. I exchanged a knowing look with her and she gave me a smile—more of a half smirk really—that confirmed what I was thinking. *At least someone else in this room is mature enough to follow such a complicated story.* That's when I also noticed something in Amber's face that I had not noticed before. I mean, when someone has just about no hair, it's hard to get past that person's no-hairness. At first, that's all you see. But now I noticed how much Amber reminded me of a flower, her mouth with its curly upper lip, her features bunched together in the center of her face.

"It's all very logical," I explained. "Point number one: Lillian's mother had been born very rich."

"Like with a fork in her mouth?" Whitney asked.

"A spoon," Amber corrected.

"Yes, a silver spoon," I went on. "Until—point number two—she had a baby—by a guy who wasn't la-de-dah like her family. Point number three: Lillian is the baby.

And finally point number four: Her rich family threw Lillian's mom out."

"Oh!" Whitney said. "Suck a duck! Suck a big, quacking duck! That makes me sore. That rich family can just kiss my skinny butt. If you say that Lillian went to live with them, man-oh-man, I won't believe it! I wouldn't let myself get adopted by people like that!"

"What about her desire?" Fern asked. "What about that?"

"Desire? Really, Fern, what are you talking about?" I said.

"Ahhhh," said the Knitting Lady. "But she did have a desire."

"To escape!" Fern said with pride. "I remembered! I'm the only one who did! So did she?"

"Y-yes, she did. But not right away. Before that . . ."

"Before that?" Monica encouraged.

"Before that, I have to s-say, must wait for another day."

⁓

I quickly discovered that one of the most unpleasant and unbearable things about living in a group home is that someone is always around, breathing the same air as you. You go into the kitchen and someone is sneaking a snack. You go to the bathroom, someone is banging on the door to get in. So while everyone else rushed outside to take a walk, I escaped to my room. It really wasn't *my* room because this wasn't my life, but it would have to do right then.

I needed to think. The Knitting Lady's story had given me so many things to think about.

For instance, Lillian had her mother. They did everything together. But did she ever wonder about her father? Did she think that someday, somewhere, a door would swing open and a man would come in and she would recognize him immediately even though they'd never met, and they wouldn't even have to be introduced because he would recognize her, too? They would just recognize each other, and he would say, *Gee, you remind me so much of me.* And she would say, *Likewise!* Did Lillian ever wonder about her father like that?

I was on my bed with a pillow propped under my head so that I could look out the window. There were some robins out there. And a tree. That's when I decided that, as long as I had to stay here, the world outside the window would belong to me. No one else had a window. Why shouldn't the outside—all of it—belong to me?

I picked up my knitting and knit a row. I knit another row. *My* tree was swaying in a light breeze. *My* cloud floated by. I knit four more rows. My stitches were definitely getting looser.

That night before I went to bed, I wrote on a piece of paper: If I were writing the story of my life, how would I begin?

I wrote: I'm in the wrong story.

When I woke the next morning, the paper was still on the floor next to my bed where I had left it. Only now, one side was covered with the prettiest handwriting I had ever seen. I never knew handwriting could be music.

Sometimes, fears come at me like genies released from a bottle.

Sometimes, I feel like everyone else has an important phone number—like God's phone number—except me.

Amber is the story of a girl who is also trying to remember.

CHAPTER 18

The next morning, I had two major accomplishments. When Whitney started talking again about her brilliant plan to look for her sister, I did *not* remind her that it was the most lame plan in the history of all lame plans ever planned. My other accomplishment was not getting on the bad side of Mrs. S., the social worker. No thanks to Whitney. Thanks to her, it was almost another story.

Our meeting started off just fine, everything under control. We were in the upstairs bedroom for "a little private tête-à-tête," as Mrs. S. called it. "I want you to feel perfectly relaxed around me," she said.

I thought: *Hot lava.*

"I want you to tell me everything's that going on around here." She was smiling so hard her gums showed.

I recited to myself: *Hot lava. Hot lava. Hot lava.*

I said nothing. I had created a new face just for the occasion. I called it My Face for Sucking Up to Social Workers, and it was almost like My Face for Unbearably Unpleasant and Embarrassing Situations, only with wider eyes. It seemed to be working. I could tell that Mrs. S. completely understood that Cal Lavender was not the type of person to spit in anyone's eye. She said, "I can tell we are going to get along just fine."

She continued the way Whitney said she would, by asking questions and more questions. *Being treated well? Getting plenty to eat?* Which I answered in complete sentences in a very mature manner. So far, so good. She nodded, wrote, and then she broke the news: I would not be going home anytime in the immediate future.

It took a lot of willpower to keep the panic from showing on My Face for Sucking Up to Social Workers. "What does the immediate future mean?" I asked. "A few more days? A week?"

Mrs. S. said that she could not give me an answer because it wasn't up to her. It was up to Betty. The social worker really emphasized that. "If Betty follows all the rules, if Betty does what she's told, if Betty makes commitments and follows through, if Betty does this and that, then—and only then—will you be released to her."

I thought, *What kind of commitments? What kind of this and that? How can anything be up to Betty? How can Betty follow rules when anyone who knows Betty knows that she can never, ever follow rules? In the life story of Betty, the first sentence would be: Betty Lavender lives to break rules. I'm the only one in the history of the universe who can get Betty to follow rules, so how will she follow them if I'm stuck here and she's stuck somewhere else?*

But I certainly didn't say any of this. My personal thoughts were none of the social worker's business. I said, "Betty will certainly follow the rules." Then I asked, "Where is she?"

Big mistake.

"You can't ask me that. A rule is a rule is a rule. And if you are even thinking about it, don't!"

"Don't what?"

"Blow this placement. Don't *think* about running away to find your mother. This is a good placement. You're lucky to have a placement this good."

I nodded with my most polite and sincere head nod. "I have a request. Whatever you do, don't put me in Whitney's fourth foster home."

Her eyes blinked twice, then widened. "Whitney!" she exclaimed. "That girl! She's a Code 600 waiting to happen."

Code 600, I reminded myself, *cold-blooded killer/ arsonist/drug-dealer types who are locked up in kid jail.*

"So," Mrs. S. probed, "what kind of malarkey has Whitney been feeding you?"

"No malarkey," I said, probably too quickly.

Her voice turned all syrupy. "Hmmm. About Whitney. Does she have any particular schemes cooking right now? Something that you are going to stay away from if you know what's good for you? So does she?"

Truthfully, I had no reason to protect Whitney. A part

of me was even thinking that I would be doing her a favor. Someone with some authority should know about her "c-r-a-z-i-e" scheme to find her sister. But the way the social worker's eyes kept scanning my face, trying to get behind my eyes and into my thoughts . . . well, it did something to me. Even though Cal Lavender is a firm believer in following the rules and even though Whitney's scheme was likely to turn into a big mess, I wasn't going to tell Mrs. S. anything. Nothing!

"No," I said. "Nothing's cooking."

The social worker hunched over some papers and started writing. I looked up. Behind Mrs. S., peeking out of the closet—guess who. Whitney, of course. How did she manage to stuff herself in there with all the clutter? She was signaling to me with hand motions like she was on a ship lost at sea. What did she want? She was making stabbing motions with her index finger.

Was she pointing at the table? Her head shook. No, not that. I pointed at the stack of files on the social worker's left.

Bingo! Okay, the files. But what did she want me to do with them?

"Don't move!" the social worker said suddenly.

I didn't. Believe me, I didn't.

Mrs. S. slowly lifted her bulk from the chair and wiggled her panty hose straight. "I need to talk to her," she said. "See if she has any questions or complaints."

I assumed she meant the Knitting Lady. "Should I come, too?" I asked.

"Wait here," she ordered, then went out the bedroom door.

Whitney charged out of the closet and began rummaging through the files that the social worker had left behind.

"What are you looking for?" I asked.

She answered, "I'm not sure." Then, "Here it is." Then, "Go stand guard."

"No," I said.

"Yes! If she catches me, you're in for it, too."

I dashed to the door and stuck my head out, looked up and down the hallway. I gave her a thumbs-up. Whitney opened a file, took out all the papers except the top few and replaced them with a stack of blank white paper.

"You can't do that!" I said. "That's got to be against the rules."

"It's my file," she hissed back. "It's got my name on it. It's all about me. Why can't I have it?" And with that, she and the papers were out the door.

I went back to the table and drummed my fingers on the top. I waited. I waited some more. I took a slow, rambling walk to the door and looked out. No one. I stood at the top of the stairs and could hear the social worker going on and on. Her voice really carried.

I charged back to the room and found the file I was

looking for. It was the fattest one there, even fatter than Whitney's. I grabbed a few papers, some from the front, the rest from the middle and back. That file, the one with Amber's name on it in block letters, was at least three inches thick.

∽

The typical average American kid has a scrapbook that her parents start putting together even before she's born. There are photographs of her mother's big belly and all the "Welcome to the World" cards from the wildly happy relatives. Over the years, the book keeps filling up—with pictures of the first birthday party, pictures of the kid when she catches her first fish and when she wore the funny Halloween costumes, and the report card with all A's and B's is there, too. The book becomes so thick that it practically splits the binding. At family parties, the book comes out and everyone sits around making comments and cracking jokes about all the honors and wonderful events that have happened in their child's life.

Amber's social-work file—the papers that I *borrowed*—was like that, only in the opposite way. It started out bad and kept getting worse. I didn't think that any life could get worse after being born in a public restroom and left to scream your head off. But Amber's life did. It started with her mother giving birth to her on the cold linoleum floor, and from there her life just seemed to get worse.

There were not a lot of details. Just a couple of lines for each time she changed foster homes and a few more lines for each time she wound up in the hospital, a part of a page for each person who hurt her and another sentence for each promise to her that was broken.

In a way, the lack of details made it even worse. It was like reading an outline for the saddest story anyone would ever write about any kid. I know I didn't see half of it. But I didn't need to. What was left out, my imagination had no trouble filling in.

I had wanted to know more about Amber. Why was she so quiet? What made her pull out her hair? What made her the way she is? Now I knew.

CHAPTER 19

I stuffed Amber's papers back under my mattress just in time. Whitney burst into the room, waving her stolen goods over her head. "Interesting! Very interesting!" she was saying. "Man-oh-man, if I didn't know this was me, I would read this stuff and think: *Now this is a* very *interesting person.* Everyone come in. You gotta hear this, too."

I couldn't look directly at Amber as she entered the room. I felt like I had just broken into her past and tiptoed around like a trespasser. She entered as quietly as someone afraid of even disturbing the dust.

Monica was next, rubbing her hands together and fretting. "I can't believe you stole those. We are going to get in so much trouble. *So* much! She's gonna find out and kill all of us."

Whitney shook an old, yellowed piece of newspaper in my face. I pushed it aside. "What's that?"

"I was"—dramatic pause—"the Child Who Waits."

What was she talking about? "The child who . . . ?"

"Who waits!" she said. "Once a month, in every newspaper in the entire county, out of all the foster kids in the entire county, they pick one kid to put in the newspaper and talk about. And in"—she stopped, ran her finger along the paper—"in May a couple years ago, I was her. I was the Child Who Waits."

I still didn't understand, so I took the paper from her and read aloud:

"'The County Department of Children's Services is looking for an adoptive family for Whitney S., a high-spirited girl of seven, small for her age because of a congenital heart problem that has been surgically corrected. Whitney is a real leader among her peers.'"

"That's right!" she said. "A real leader."

"'She has a very well-developed imagination.'"

"Told you that's me!"

I continued, "'After experiencing severe abuse by her parents, she has lived in several foster homes and has had to deal with feelings of abandonment and a lack of a stable family environment.'"

"Well, that's not entirely wrong. Go on," she said.

"'Because of her difficult childhood, Whitney can tend to live in a fantasy world. She would best be served by a patient, well-grounded family with other children to help—'"

"What do they mean? Living in a fantasy world? I don't—"

"'—with other children to help satisfy her immense longing for siblings.'"

"And what the heck is a sibling?" she asked.

"A sister. Or a brother," I answered.

Whitney grabbed the paper and sneered at it. "What do they know? I don't need somebody else's sibling. I already have one of my own. I just have to find her." Whitney whirled to face me. "And now I have all the clues I need." She patted the pile of social-work papers. "Everything I need."

"Let me see!" Monica demanded.

Whitney's voice lowered. "Not yet, but soon. And it all depends."

"On what?" I asked.

"If all of you are going to help me find her."

Amber was nodding rapidly. Yes, of course she would help. Even timid, tired-all-the-time, scaredy-cat Monica with a broken arm was saying yes. And if *she* said yes, I knew that Fern, her personal shadow, would also go along with it.

As a group, they turned and looked at me.

Luckily, I didn't have to answer yes or no because the door flung open and Fern was standing there waving her needles. "She said to bring your knitting and come down. She's ready to tell the next part of the story."

Like I said, I didn't say anything, but I could tell from the satisfied look that Whitney gave me that I might as well have said, *Yes! Cal Lavender will help you with your nutty plan!*

"Do you like the story so far?" the Knitting Lady asked.

The answer seemed important to her. "A lot," Fern said.

"I'm s-so glad because I always worry that, with my stutter, I never do the stories justice. When I was your age, I hated that I stuttered. I hated that I hated that I stuttered. Then I hated that I hated that I hated that I stuttered. Which just seemed to make me stutter even more. Even now, at my age, after a lifetime of stuttering, I can't stop looking at my listeners and asking myself: *Do I look stupid when I talk? Are they bored? Am I taking too long to tell it?*"

"But you hardly stutter at all when you're telling a story," I said.

"Especially this story," Whitney added.

"I th-think I also noticed that. It's like something outside of myself comes along and unloosens the knot from my tongue. This must be a pretty important story for something like that to happen. Still, I worry that . . ."

"Don't worry so much," Whitney said. "Just tell the story."

The Knitting Lady gave a little snort of amusement. "So I will. Do you remember where we left off?"

"The dead mother." Monica shivered at the memory. "How could I forget?"

"Escape, something about escape," Fern added.

Amber was very precise: "Suspended in the air, nothing solid under her feet."

"Y-yes. After that day, after her mother was buried, Lillian was passed around from one rich cousin to another like a puppy no one wanted. Then one day, the Reverend sat before Lillian, took her by the hand.

"'So, young lady,' he said, 'have you ever traveled before?'

"And Lillian said, 'Damn straight, I've been all over the Lower East Side of New York.'"

At that, we all cracked up because the Knitting Lady was a good mimic, and it sounded exactly like something Whitney would say.

"You laugh, but I can t-tell you that the Reverend did not see the humor one little bit. He looked like he was choking on a chicken bone. The Reverend was of the belief that children are innocent jewels, and it shook him to his very core to hear a little girl swearing like a sailor. You girls and I know that cussing never killed anyone, but that's not the way this man thought. His whole purpose in life was to rescue poor, cussing, orphaned waifs like Lillian.

"'Well, young lady,' he continued, 'now you are *really* going to do some traveling—far from New York City. Most people just dream of heading west. But you are going to join with other lucky boys and girls just like yourself, to be part of the biggest migration of children that the world has ever known.'

"The Reverend was a man of the church, but he spoke like a salesman. Escape! Adventure! He told Lillian that she would have the opportunity to ride ponies, which for a city girl was like promising a rocket trip to Mars. She would be whisked away on a train to a place where the air was so clean, she could run for miles without coughing. And there would be so much food—not just cabbage and more cabbage like she was used to, but fresh milk and cakes that dripped with honey and chocolate.

"He said to her, 'Don't you want to learn how to milk a cow? Don't you want to get a good upbringing and learn to speak a refined English? Out west, you will learn to churn butter and stitch quilts.'

"About churning and quilting, Lillian knew nothing. But when the Reverend started speaking of dresses— pretty, fancy, new dresses, not rags like she was used to wearing—he tapped into her deepest fantasy. Her eyes began rolling to the top of her head like Dorothy in the field of poppies. She practically swooned as he spoke of calico prints, gingham, and satin sashes.

"It was all so much like a fairy tale coming true that Lillian did not think to ask certain questions. Like, What did the Reverend mean by *boys and girls like her*? Or,

Why would people Lillian had never met want to drape her in gingham dresses?

"So when the Reverend asked, 'So, you lucky little girl, what do you say to this blessed opportunity?' what could Lillian say? She had never been so intoxicated! Suddenly her mother's death was the furthest thing from her mind.

"No! That's not quite true. Nobody's mother's death is ever the furthest thing from her mind. But Lillian did not really, truly understand that dead means you are never, ever going to see the dead person again. 'Heck yes!' she said. 'I want to go.'

"After that, so much happened so fast. Strangers scrubbed Lillian until her skin felt raw. They probed her ears and dug around in her nose. As the Reverend had said, a lot of boys and girls had been rounded up for this great trip west. Like Lillian, each one assumed they had been especially selected, but it was just a matter of their circumstances. A parent's death. A desertion. Some had committed a minor crime. Maybe they stole some apples. In those days, many children went to jail just for stealing a few lumps of coal.

"While getting ready for the trip, they all lived together for a short period in a building that was like a group home, only this one was twelve stories high and packed with children! Some were so skinny that their shoulder blades stuck out like wishbones, and most balked at being put into clothes that were tight-necked and scratchy as burlap.

"But not Lillian. Lillian loved all the attention.

"*Stand up straight.* She stood up straight.

"*Don't scratch.* She stopped scratching.

"*Smile. Curtsy when introduced. Lower your eyes in modesty.* Noted, noted, noted. Lillian practiced her 'Yes, ma'am's and 'No, sir's and did not even fuss when a cranky woman with a comb pulled and tore at the knots in her long, thick hair.

"Finally the big day arrived. Just before noon, a large group of children were led into a great, empty hall and lined up in rows. Each child held a suitcase. The boys were so clean in their short pants and cotton broadcloth shirts buttoned high around their necks. All the girls were wearing new dresses. Lillian studied the back of the thin, red-haired girl in front of her. She was holding the hand of a dark-haired little boy and had six perfect curls hanging like sausages around her head.

"In front of the room, the Reverend walked back and forth. 'A clean slate,' he kept repeating, each time with more force. He patted heads and straightened collars, and, when he finally stopped pacing and gestured for the children to start moving out, he was standing directly in front of Lillian.

"Well, that did it! Lillian decided that it wasn't by chance that the leader of this whole expedition stopped right in front of her. This was a sign! She must be the one who was most destined for a life that was wonderful and marvelous!

"When the lines of children started moving, Lillian followed the girl in front of her onto the streets of New York. People looked at them as they passed. Lillian tossed her freshly washed and combed hair. She flashed each stranger a smile. She was sure they were wondering: *Who is that immaculate child who walks in such a straight line? Where is she going? How I envy her!*

"All the way to the train station, Lillian dug her nails into the flesh of her thigh to keep from breaking into song. What a train ride it was to be!"

CHAPTER 20

The Knitting Lady shifted in her chair and continued. "There were fifty children accompanied by five adults who were leaving by train from New York City that day. The children had never seen anything like Grand Central Station. There were pillars of marble as thick and mottled as tree trunks. Steel posts rose a hundred feet high. Picture the long lines of track, the confusion and excitement of trains pulling out. Put yourself in the children's brand-new shoes. They covered their ears as train whistles blew. That's our train! All aboard! The children were hustled up the steps, the smallest ones tucked under arms like suitcases to be carried aboard.

"'Best day of my life,' one boy kept saying. And another: 'Hip, hip, hurrah for the Wild West!' The train lurched. Everyone squealed as it picked up speed.

"As I said earlier, the children had been told that it was going to be a long journey, but they didn't grasp the full meaning of that. Many had never set foot outside of their neighborhoods, so some thought *long* meant they were going to New Jersey, just across the river. One girl took to heart the Reverend's description. Pure air and all the food she could eat. *Why,* she thought, *this train must be going to heaven.*

"At first, there was so much energy. The antsy children couldn't sit still. The talky ones couldn't get their words out fast enough. But eventually, the rocking of the train, the grinding hum of the rail, wore them all down. One after another, the children took on a brain-dazed look, like baby birds who had been pushed from the nest for the first time."

"But not Lillian," I said. "She wouldn't look dazed."

"W-why not, Cal?"

"Because she wouldn't want anyone to know what she was feeling inside."

"Exactly! S-she was in a window seat, next to an agent, one of the adults who were paid to accompany the children. One of Lillian's hands was in the pocket of her dress and she was clasping something. Take a guess, what?"

"A snack!" Monica said. "That's what I would have taken. You know how I'm always hungry. And if I didn't eat on a train, I know I'd get train sick."

"N-no, not a snack. Here's a clue: It was something she wasn't supposed to have. Hold that clue awhile. It'll come to you. Many hours passed, and Lillian's head began to loll. She jerked herself awake, then drifted off again, slumping against the agent next to her. This woman in her dark blue suit removed Lillian's head from her shoulder, like it was a muddy thing. Then, she straightened her own small hat. I bet each of you would recognize the woman, how her eyes were always taking measure. That's right, Whitney, she was like a social worker of that time.

"So Lillian drifted in and out of sleep. When awake, she saw things out the window that a city girl would not have names for. Forests, silos, fallow fields. Once when she woke, the train was stopped at a station. She had never seen so much space or anything look as lonely as that one wooden building set against a backdrop of sky.

"Other times, Lillian slept right through the stops, only vaguely aware of movement and that the train always felt lighter. At some point, she realized why. At each stop, some of the children got off and the train moved on without them. It was always the children who had placards hanging around their necks."

"Placards?" I asked.

"Oh!" the Knitting Lady said. "I forgot to tell you all about the placards!" She demonstrated by wrapping a piece of yarn loosely around her neck. "The placards were pieces of cardboard that hung on string just like this. Before getting on the train, an agent hung placards on some of the children. Most of the babies—teeny, khaki-colored, scowling things—had numbers pinned to their bonnets. Lillian didn't get a number, but the girl in line in front of her—the red-haired girl with the six sausage-shaped curls—was number thirty-four."

Whitney shouted out: "Question! Was the redheaded girl special because she *had* a number? Or was Lillian special because she *didn't* have one?"

"Those are the s-same questions that were driving Lillian crazy."

Whitney went on, "And how about the dark-haired boy holding her hand? Did he have a tag?"

"There's no dark-haired boy in this story," Fern insisted.

Whitney said, "Oh, yes, there is. He's holding the hand of Miss Sausage Hair."

"G-good memory, Whitney. The dark-haired boy is her brother."

Fern broke in: "So Lillian had a brother?"

The Knitting Lady explained patiently, "No, the brother belonged to the red-haired girl. And no, he did not have a tag. Lillian could read, so she put her mind to figuring out what was written on the girl's placard. First, there was her name—*Rosie*—and then her age—*7. Red hair. Green eyes. Very quiet and hopeful.* There was something else written there—*Trenton, Mo.*—but Lillian couldn't make sense of it.

"It wasn't until the fourth day of the trip, after the train crossed a big river and pulled into yet another station, that the words *Trenton, Mo.,* made sense. Those were the same words that were written on the station platform. Lillian pressed her face against the window and watched as all of the children with 'Trenton, Mo.' on their placards exited the train.

"By this point in their travels, the children were a far cry from the clean and spotless children who had boarded in New York City. The older ones looked numb from being cooped up for so long, and you all know how toddlers can get just looking at dirt. Well, you never saw a toddler as wrinkled and stained as number 30! But a woman holding a sign with NUMBER 30 written on it stepped out of the crowd waiting on the platform. She rushed forward waving wildly and then scooped up number 30 like the child was a lottery prize. All around, similar scenes were taking place.

"*I signed up for number 15!*

"*That cute little 21 is mine!*

"In the middle of all the confusion, Rosie, number 34, was standing and looking as bewildered as if she had just been dropped, suitcase and all, right from outer space. Kaboom!

"A man wearing farmer's overalls and a woman wearing a faded flowered housedress stepped out of the crowd. They were holding a sign: 34. The man walked up to an agent, put out his hand, and they did one of those long, slow, serious pumping handshakes. The farmer pointed to

Rosie. The woman's hand reached out toward Rosie's hair, then pulled back suddenly as if she were too hot to touch.

"Lillian pulled on the sleeve of the agent sitting next to her. 'What's that man saying?'

"The woman bristled. 'Don't point! And don't pull! If you want to be picked, you best mind your manners.'

"Lillian didn't understand. 'Then why are they picking her? She's not doing a curtsy or smiling or anything good-mannered.'

"The agent's body made a sharp movement like she just experienced a twinge of heartburn. 'That girl doesn't have to do anything right. They asked for a red-haired, green-eyed seven-year-old girl, and the bill was filled. Just like they ordered her from the Sears Catalogue.'

"As Lillian watched, her eyes went soft with a feeling of embarrassment."

"Embarrassment?" I asked. "Why would she be embarrassed?"

"Th-that is the question, isn't it? Lillian did nothing wrong."

The Knitting Lady looked pointedly around the room, set her eyes on each of us in turn. When she got to Whitney, her eyes held a little longer.

"Because she figured something must be wrong with her," Whitney said.

"Why, Whitney? Explain why Lillian w-would think something was wrong with her."

"Because she wasn't picked," Whitney answered sharply. "Why else didn't she get picked? Because something is wrong with her."

It didn't make any sense to me why Whitney was acting so agitated. It was just a story. "It's just a story, Whitney," I said.

I waited for Whitney to snap something back, but for once, she didn't. She didn't seem angry at me in particular. She seemed angry at everyone and everything.

The Knitting Lady picked up her needles and started knitting as she spoke. "That's true, Cal. It's a story. But Whitney understands what Lillian was feeling. It's no different from today, is it? Certain children are adopted because they just happen to have a certain color hair or they are a certain age or sex."

Now I understood, and it *was* unfair! "Just because someone has red hair! What's the big deal about that? There's nothing wrong with Lillian."

The Knitting Lady was nodding. "But how do you think Lillian felt, sitting there behind a glass window, watching one child after another being claimed as if they were valuable jewels?"

"Really, really bad," Monica said. "I bet she started crying. I would. I feel like crying right now just thinking about it."

"But Lillian would never cry," I said. "I bet she had a face to put on just for moments like this one."

"B-but she felt like crying, certainly. At that moment, Lillian was struck by a fit of longing to see her mother's face. She had to see it, feel her mother's eyes passing over her with love and approval. But there was no mother. *I am alone,* she thought. *Really, really alone.*

"The train began moving again. There were not many children left aboard. Holding back tears, Lillian looked out and saw Rosie standing on the platform, a finger wedged between her lips, her hair like a flame on a slender white candle.

"In the front of the train, one of the other unclaimed children—the little dark-haired boy, Rosie's brother—started wailing."

"That makes me so mad, I want to punch someone," Whitney said. Her whole body was twitching. "Why didn't that farmer take Rosie *and* her brother? People should not be allowed to split up . . . split up— Amber, what shouldn't they be allowed to split up?"

"Siblings," Amber said quietly.

"I d-don't know the answer to your question, Whitney. That's the way it happened. Lillian thought Rosie was lucky, but how lucky was she? To be taken from her brother? For her brother to be taken from her?

"When the station was out of sight, the agent next to Lillian gave a shudder and fell asleep. Now it was safe for Lillian to reach into her pocket and take out her smuggled treasure."

"What treasure?" Fern asked.

"Yeah, I forgot about that," Monica put in. "Something in her pocket."

"Any g-guesses what it is? Cal?"

"I don't know."

"Amber?"

She did not hesitate. "The fancy French glasses."

"Correct! The l-lorgnette. And what do you suppose she did with the glasses, Amber?"

Amber closed her eyes and said, "Lillian ran her fingers over the pieces of glass."

"Yes," the Knitting Lady said, "and as she held the lorgnette, she felt herself being rejected by her neighbors in New York, her rich relatives, and now by the people of Trenton, Missouri. She felt the desertion of a father she never knew. She saw her mother's face fading feature by feature and knew that, one day, she would barely be able to remember her mother at all. Sadness, hurt, anger, and fear. For the next few hours, she wrestled with these feelings and pinned them down like they were wild animals. She tamed them into something else."

"What?" Fern asked.

"Vows. That d-day on the train, Lillian made three vows:

1. Nobody will ever hurt me again.
2. Someday, everyone will know my name.
3. My life will never be ordinary. It will be spectacular.

"In her window seat, she pulled her back up straight and sat aloof like some kind of untouchable queen. Lillian held her mother's lorgnette to her face. The scenery rushed by. She used this very last piece of her past to look forward into her future."

"And then?" I asked.

"And then . . . and then . . . for the next part of Lillian's story, there's always another day."

CHAPTER 21

"I have vows, too," Whitney said to me. Her face started twitching and winking, like it was being bombarded by small jolts of electricity. Whitney might as well have been wearing a neon sign that said, *I've got a secret!*

The Knitting Lady told us that this was enough story-telling for one day. "Go over to the park. Run off some steam."

We were out the door and halfway up the street when Whitney started looking around for intergalactic spies. Finding none, she decided it was safe to bring up her supersecret subject—her *only* subject. "My vow is to find her this month."

"Her?" Fern asked, and Monica rolled her eyes, and Fern said, "Oh, *her.*"

Whitney rubbed her palms together and laughed like a mad scientist in a bad horror movie. "I have all the necessary information in my hungry little hands."

When we got to Horace Mann Middle School, she insisted that we take a detour onto the deserted campus where she proceeded to point out a million things that I had no reason to care about. Over there was the door where she, *not I,* would enter on the first day of school. The portable on the right was the office where she, *not I,* would meet the principal. Under the large tree was where she, *not I,* would eat lunch every day.

After I got the complete and unnecessary tour of a school I cared nothing about, Whitney returned to her previous subject. "So, you're all taking off with me, right." It wasn't even a question. "You're all coming with me on this mission. Man-oh-man, it's gonna be great."

At least I could count on Monica to be a wimp. "The Knitting Lady will be mad!" she said, and I kept encouraging her. "How can you take off with your arm in a cast?" and "Think how tired you'll get!" and "Mrs. S. will have a fit when she finds out!" Monica kept nodding in agreement with me, but I also noticed how her eyes started darting back and forth to Whitney. Then the nodding stopped. Whitney didn't even say anything, she didn't have to. In the list of things that Monica was afraid of, getting on Whitney's bad side was high up there.

"Okay, count me in," Monica finally agreed.

Fern giggled and gave the thumbs-up sign, although I'm not really sure that she understood exactly what she was agreeing to do.

And of course Amber was with Whitney all the way.

"So where *is* your sister?" Monica asked. "Is it far? I

hope we don't have to walk far 'cause, you know, I don't like getting all sweaty and—"

Whitney broke in. Her expression was mysterious. "It's far. That's all I can say for now. The details will be revealed at the appropriate time."

Meanwhile, I was thinking: *Maybe, just maybe, the appropriate time will be NEVER. Yes, that would be exactly like Whitney. She was definitely the all-talk type. In any case, I will absolutely refuse to go because that is exactly the same as running away, which is exactly what the social worker ordered me not to do under any circumstances. Don't even consider it! And didn't Whitney herself say to hurl myself into hot lava before getting on the wrong side of Mrs. S.?*

I also thought: *Who are those girls who have been walking behind us for blocks? Why are they following us and pretending not to?*

When we got to the playground, the girls stood off from us in a huddle at the top of the climbing structure. There was a tall one who poked the skinny one who shook her head no. Then, a girl wearing a belly shirt pointed to a girl in a pink tank top who mouthed, *Not me*. Then they seemed to all turn at once to a girl with flippy hair, who shrugged like she had known all along that they would get around to her. She jumped on the fireman's pole, slid down, and walked toward us. She was trying to act like it was no big deal, but I noticed that she kept turning around and looking back to her friends for support. When she was right in front of Whitney, she flipped her flippy hair and said: "You go to Horace Mann, right?"

"Righto," Whitney said back.

"You all eat lunch together under the tree, right?"

"Righto."

"We thought so," she said. "We were wondering . . ." Another look back at her friends. "We've seen you around. We were wondering . . . like . . . who you are?"

"Whitney," Whitney answered.

"No. I mean, what are you?"

Whitney snapped, "What's that mean?"

"Hey, don't get mad. It's just that everyone wants to know. You live in that orange house. And you're always together, but you can't be sisters or cousins, right? I mean, you're so pale." She paused and pointed to me. "And she's so dark. . . ." Then she pointed to Amber, but changed her mind and pointed to Monica instead. "And she's so big. And you're all the same age, so you can't be sisters."

Whitney said quickly, "We're friends. Like you and your friends."

Flippy Hair dismissed that immediately. "No, that can't be it. Friends don't live in the same house." She turned and pointed to her friends who looked scared that we might bite. "We don't get it. We just don't get it."

"I have two questions," I asked the Knitting Lady as soon as I got back to the Pumpkin House. "What are we?"

"A tribe," she said. "Second question?"

"Did your hands get like that from knitting?"

She put down the yarn and spread her hands flat on her thighs. The veins were thick, and I had to stop myself from reaching out and pressing one of those plump worms. "I g-guess they are big and muscular compared to the pint-sized rest of me. But did I get them from knitting? Hmmm. That's hard to say. I've been knitting a long time. I remember when I first started, my hands would cramp up something fierce." She wiggled her fingers.

"Your hands used to hurt?" I exclaimed. "Mine hurt, too. I thought I was doing something wrong. So I'm not doing anything wrong?"

She gave me a funny look. "If I was going to tell the story of your life, know how I'd start it? *Cal Lavender worries way too much about doing something wrong.* You and Monica have a lot in common that way. Let's see what the Stitch Reader can see."

I handed my knitting to her, and she let out a long, approving whistle. I have to admit that my knitting was pretty impressive. Nobody else knit first thing in the morning and last thing at night like I did. My work had a lot of sun colors in it, yellows and golds, and was already three times as long as anybody else's.

"So what do you see in my knitting now?" I asked her. "Much looser, right?"

She pulled the material gently and watched it spring back into shape. "A nice, even h-hand. There's a calmness to it. Uh-oh. Here."

She had homed right in on one of my few mistakes. A couple of stitches had somehow gotten tangled together. "What were you thinking when you were working on this row?"

"Nothing. I wasn't thinking. I was just knitting. And listening to your story."

"What part of the story?"

"I don't know! How am I supposed to know? I don't remember!"

She didn't ask anything else. I slid my finger along the stitches, then pressed my fingertip gently into the point of the needle. I said, "Let's say that *for instance,* I did remember. Not that I do! But let's say that I did. What would it mean?"

"It means that right here"—she lifted my finger from the point and placed it on the twisted row—"right here, your mind was not at peace. Does that make sense?"

"Sure," I said, "*if* I could remember. Which I definitely cannot!"

～

Okay, so I could remember. I knew exactly what the Knitting Lady was saying when my hands lost their way. She was saying that Lillian *was watching her mother's face fade feature by feature.*

CHAPTER 22

Possible opening sentences for "The Cal Lavender Story" by Cal Lavender:

> Cal Lavender will never let her mother's face fade feature by feature.
> Cal Lavender worries way too much about doing something wrong.
> Cal Lavender vows that she won't let Whitney talk her into doing anything stupid.
> Cal Lavender vows she will be the best knitter the Knitting Lady has ever seen.

It was very strange, but I started seeing Lillian everywhere.

Whenever we were riding in the van, I sat in the back and studied the shape of Amber's head. I said to myself: *I bet Lillian's head was shaped like that.* When Monica acted fearful, when Fern seemed to be in another world, I knew that Lillian sometimes felt those ways, too, even though she would never show it.

When everyone was asleep, I looked out my window and saw the silhouettes of the spindly rosebushes on the patio. The shadows cast by the moonlight looked like her. I knew that if it was day and I was looking out this same window, clouds would drift by in the form of Lillian walking, Lillian dancing, Lillian making her vows.

CHAPTER 23

I had an important question that I could not get out of my mind. I found the Knitting Lady and everyone else in Talk Central. "Who's the best knitter in the Pumpkin House?" I asked.

"And don't do that thing that grown-ups always do!" Whitney put in. "Don't say that everyone is the best in her own way, blah-blah. Nobody falls for that kind of bull."

The Knitting Lady laughed. "I wouldn't do that."

Whitney pointed to Monica. "It can't be her because she won't even try knitting."

"I can't do it! I don't know how, and, anyway, it hurts my hands."

Then Monica pointed to Fern. "And it can't be her because she's always losing her knitting and starting over. Fern, have you ever finished anything?"

"I don't think so," Fern said.

"Who's the best then?" Whitney asked.

There was not even an "Ahhh" before the Knitting Lady answered. "That's easy. Amber."

Amber was peeking up through her bangs-that-aren't-there, as surprised as the rest of us to be named Miss Pumpkin House Knitter of the Year. It dawned on me that I had never seen any of Amber's finished work. Whitney burst out, "You've got to be kidding. Man alive, Amber is the *worst* knitter."

Monica agreed. "No offense, Amber, but you are."

Whitney addressed me: "Have you ever seen what she does?" Then she turned to the Knitting Lady. "Oh, you're joking. I get it now."

"I'm not j-joking. Amber, go get some of my favorites."

Amber came back with full hands and set them out on the coffee table. There were five small, doll-sized things. A little sweater. A yellow cap. A knitted pair of pants. Talk about the need to be *loose, loose.* The knitting was so tight, each item stood up on its own like a little piece of armor.

But tight was only the beginning of the problem. I picked up the little sweater. It had a nice pattern that must have been very hard to do without losing her peace of mind. It was pink and red, but with three sleeves and no opening for the head.

Every piece was like that! Absolutely perfect and perfectly wrong! The pants were joined at the cuffs so that you'd have to be shaped like a circle to wear them. The cap came to a sharp alien-head point. The dress was a complete and total success, but only if you happened to have six arms and a giraffe neck.

I said, "Nobody can wear these. Therefore, she can't be the best knitter."

Amber looked hurt. Her hands started rubbing the back of her neck. I also noticed that thin wisps of reddish-brown hair had begun to sprout all over her head. She looked like a newly hatched bird.

The Knitting Lady gently removed Amber's hands from her hair and made a cup of them. "My favorite," she said, indicating the dress in the center. "Totally impractical, Cal. But that's the beauty of it."

The beauty of it? Amber's knitting broke all the rules, or what I thought were the rules. How was I, Cal Lavender, supposed to become the best knitter if the rules changed for each person? I asked, "After Amber, then, who would you say is the best knitter?"

"I'm the fastest knitter," Whitney bragged.

"And the messiest," I pointed out.

"Well, la-de-dah!"

The Knitting Lady kicked off her shoes, bent over, and rubbed her feet. "Squabbling. Is that the only cure for boredom around here?"

"No, telling a story!" Whitney insisted. "That'll make us stop."

"Lillian!" Monica said.

"Where did we l-leave her?"

I had the answer. "Riding the train into her future."

"What does she have with her?"

"The lorgnette," Fern said, proud that she remembered.

"And what else does she h-have?"

We yelled out the first things that popped into our heads: *Shoes! Toothbrush! A suitcase!* It was Amber who said, "Vows."

"Th-that's the answer I was looking for. She's on the train and there's an important stop coming up. The agent next to Lillian told her to tidy herself up the best she could. *Straighten the bow on your dress. Put on a smile.*

" 'What happens if no one picks me?' Lillian asked.

" 'Someone will.' Only the way the agent said it, f-flatly without any enthusiasm or flattery, didn't give Lillian much hope.

" 'But what if they don't?' she asked.

" 'Then, you get put back on the train and returned to New York. And where would you be then? So don't make trouble.'

CHAPTER 24

"Ten children," the Knitting Lady continued, "all that were left of the original fifty, stepped off the train that afternoon. Girls in disheveled dresses looking as rumpled as used wrapping paper. Boys with greasy hair as though it had been ironed flat on their heads. The agents advised them to step lively, to appear energetic and self-reliant, but they mostly lumbered off like cattle, stiff in the joints, tired and bewildered from so many claustrophobic days on the train.

"Two teenage girls held hands. A tall boy protectively wrapped an arm around Rosie's little brother. Even arch-enemies stood close to each other, blinking through the haze and dust at the throng of strangers gathered to see them. Across the platform, a man with a peculiar way of walking stepped out of the crowd and headed their way.

"Lillian was the only one standing off by herself, her attention focused on some cattle grazing by the tracks. Were these the cows the Reverend had told her she would learn to milk? She felt a jolt of disappointment that they looked so dull and stupid.

"*So this is the Wild West,* she thought. She didn't know what she had expected.

"Oh, yes, she did! She had expected everything: things that were shiny and new, acres of satin and lace for dresses, trees blossoming with honey cakes. The train had left New York in the height of a sticky, choking summer, and she was now standing in something even worse. Nebraska heat can fry anybody's nerves to the flash point."

"Tell about the man!" Whitney demanded. "The one with the wacky walk."

"You r-really homed in on him. Good instincts. He's an important part of the story. Mr. R. M. Tankersley was a chicken farmer. The area was full of such gruff, barrel-chested men who had been toughened by work and weather.

"To look at him, Mr. R. M. Tankersley may have appeared to be a man without a lot of inner feelings. But he was a man who loved his wife so fully and deeply that he was ready to do anything for her, no matter how desperate and impractical.

"Several weeks earlier, Mr. Tankersley had spotted posters announcing the impending arrival of the children from New York City. Those posters got him thinking. Maybe, just maybe, one of the train children would be the key to solving his problem."

WANTED! HOMES FOR CHILDREN
A company of homeless children
from the East will be arriving.

These children are of various ages and of both sexes,
having been thrown friendless upon the world.
The citizens of this community are asked to assist
the agent, MISS CHARLOTTE FRY, in securing
good homes for them. Persons taking these
children must be approved by the local committee.
They must treat the children in every way
as a member of the family.

A VIEWING AND DISTRIBUTION WILL BE MADE AT THE OPERA HOUSE.

"For weeks now, there had been such notices posted all around town. It seemed to be all the citizens could talk about. *What kind of children are these? Did they have immoral parents?* Even those who had no intention of taking in a child showed up at the train station to peek at the unfortunates.

"In crowds, Mr. Tankersley was usually painfully shy. He knew that about himself, so all morning before the train arrived, he sat out by his chicken coops, taking long, slow drinks of blueberry wine, a way of building up his courage. And now he was walking across on the train platform, his mouth stained a deep, brownish-purple. Despite the alcohol, his eyes held a sharp focus as he scanned the children. He automatically ruled out the boys. A boy wouldn't do at all. So that left only five to choose from. *No, not that girl or that one either.* He looked over each in turn, making dissatisfied little clicks with his tongue. None could hold a candle to what he needed.

"Then he focused in on Lillian. She was wrong by a mile—wrong age, wrong coloring—but his eyes kept coming back to her. Perhaps he was drawn to the way she held herself apart from the others. In any case, he walked his peculiar walk right up and asked in her face, 'Girly, you have good eyes?'

"The man made Lillian feel turned upside down like a carnival ride. Despite all her practicing for just this moment, she was barely able to whisper a single word: 'Eyes?'

" 'Good eyes?' he responded.

" 'Good?'

"The man drew himself up. 'What's the matter with you, girl? You a parrot? What are you hiding in there? Open up now, let's see them teeth.' His hand, like a rough claw, latched on to her jaw. 'Come on, girly. My mind is set on this, but I can't afford no one whose dentaltry's not sound.'

"She felt a thick salty finger take a commanding sweep around her gums, over the bumpy surface of her tongue and the points of her canine teeth. When the finger ran over the gully of her right molar, she remembered vow number one. Which is . . ."

"No one will ever hurt me," I said.

"So Lillian bit down. Hard. The man let out a shocked, whooping yell. Our Lillian was furious. Mr. Tankersley, who was yelling, 'The little rascal bit me!' was furious, too. The crowd was furious. You could tell by all the stern chins jutting in Lillian's direction. The agent— Miss Charlotte Fry—rushed over. To Lillian, she hissed, 'Have you taken leave of your senses?'

"Then she turned to Mr. Tankersley and, without extending her hand, said: 'Miss Charlotte Fry, agent for these children. And you are?'

"'R. M. Tankersley. Anyone here can vouch for me.'

"'I'm sure they can.' Miss Charlotte Fry drew a deep breath, getting a clear whiff of alcohol. 'But there are procedures, sir. You can't walk up and take a child. That's why we're gathering in the Opera House. If you're still interested—'

"'I'm interested.' He was sucking on his finger. 'I'm interested.'

"Several men sidled up to Tankersley and tried in their awkward farmer ways to make light of the episode. Their wives felt very protective of Tankersley because of all his troubles at home. They turned their cold comments on Lillian:

"Shame on her!

"Took leave of her senses, all right!

"She is the homeliest, most unpromising girl in the whole lot.

"Incorrigible! It's the blood that tells.

"A few moments later, the children were led away from the station. They made quite a sight, walking single file past the feed and grain store, the library, the post office, the newspaper office, toward the Opera House. The townspeople, including R. M. Tankersley, followed in a pack behind them. He kept his eyes on the back of Lillian, the way her shoulders were still thin but square, the way they never slumped.

ᥱ

"Sitting on chairs on the stage of the Opera House, the girls kept their legs crossed daintily at the ankles as they had been coached; the boys had hats on their laps. At the podium, Mayor Clyde Shook gestured with the full length of his arm. 'Our great need today, fellow citizens, are strong hands and hearts willing to take in one of these homeless waifs. The Society that sent these children says that the lot of them has had good discipline. I personally felt the arm of this fine young man behind me. His eyes may be a little crossed, but he would be mighty useful on the farm.'

"'Mayor Shook! Mayor Shook! I have a question about these youngsters!'

"'Who is that yelling out? Ah, a Hazeltine. Margaret, why don't you pose your question loud enough so the balcony can hear you. Don't be shy!'

"The plain, round-faced woman stood and made a megaphone of her right fist, 'Here's my question. Let's say we're thinking it would be a nice gesture to open our doors to one of these orphans. But say, when we get the little fella home, well, people have different ways. What if the little fella can't undo his upbringing, if you see where I'm headed with this?'

"'That's a good question Margaret poses,' the mayor said. 'The lady sitting here to my right, Miss Charlotte Fry, gave me her solemn assurances that if you and your orphan don't get along, an official agent will come right on over to your place and take that child back.'

"'Is there a charge for any of this?'

"'No ma'am. Your child comes free on a ninety-day trial basis. Does that answer your questions, Margaret?'

"'Yes sir, it does. I already have five daughters at home, so I'll take that little fella over there, third one in. Bet he can handle chores and a half—especially after I fatten him up with my cooking.'

"Another voice came out of the crowd: 'Hold it there, Margaret. I had my eye on that one. Mayor Shook, not fair, just because—'

" 'Hold on here, folks. We don't want to go pitting neighbor against neighbor. I believe Miss Charlotte Fry wants to say a few words.'

"The agent stood and walked to center stage. 'All this enthusiasm is very encouraging. But it is no light matter taking an unknown child into your home. There's been a committee appointed of your own townspeople to approve each match. And even when the committee approves a family, that does not end it. The child also has a say in the matter. Any child who doesn't want to go with a particular family does not have to go. And any child who wants to leave a family has that right. Any questions?'

"Fifty adult hands shot up, and one child's hand, Lillian's. The mayor showed the audience his own palms. 'Now, folks, why don't we just get started, and I'm betting that questions get resolved along the way. We might as well begin with the little fella that Margaret has her eye on. No catfights now, ladies. Young man, come forward.'

"The child in question was seated next to Lillian, and when he didn't budge, she gave him a good pinch. Still, the child didn't move. Only when the mayor himself came over—'Come on, son. No one's gonna bite you'—did the child finally stand. The mayor kept prodding, 'That's right, son, a few more steps into the spotlight, good boy. What's your name, son?'

"But before the child could answer, the Hazeltine

woman shouted, 'You wanna come home with me, little boy? The Hazeltines will give you your own pony.'

"Still the child didn't speak, which made the audience buzz with speculation.

"Bet that boy has a screw loose!

"His ears must be clogged with New York dirt!

"Bet he speaks only one of those gutter foreign tongues, not a lick of English!

"But the child was clearly neither deaf nor stupid. There was definitely a whole lot of something going on behind those eyes. When he finally gathered up what he had to say, his hands were balled into little fists.

"He shouted, 'I ain't no widdle boy! I'm a widdle girl!'

"Well, that caused a sensation! People gasped. Some started laughing so hard their eyes rolled to the top of their heads. Agent Fry frantically thumbed through a stack of papers, and only when she found the right one did she admit the mistake: 'He's right. I mean, *she's* right. He IS a girl! It says so right here.'

"The mayor asked, 'Young lady, what happened to your dress?'

"'Can't tell,' the girl said.

"'Don't be disobedient. You want one of these nice people to take you home?'

"The girl dropped her chin to the dimple of her neck. 'I went and—'

"'Speak up. We can't hear you.'

"'I said'—and now she was shouting—'I went and peed my dress. So Charlie over there slipped me these britches from his suitcase.'

"Well, that got everyone as giddy as confetti, and the mayor took advantage of the high spirits. 'No harm done, right, folks? This is one resourceful little gal. Spunky! Margaret, I suppose you'll pass. You got enough females at your place.'

"But Mrs. Hazeltine was already rushing down the aisle, squealing at the top of her lungs, 'Oh, isn't she the most precious? Of course I want her.'

"The girl in the boy clothes asked, 'Can I have a pony even if I am a girl?' And when Mrs. Hazeltine said, 'Of course, of course,' the child flung herself off the stage like a bouquet into the woman's open arms.

"The townspeople had certainly seen some very touching theatrical scenes performed on that stage. But never had they witnessed anything as all-around emotionally satisfying as what had just transpired. After that, there was one happy ending after another. The mayor announced: 'Eleven-year-old Chas F. Doesn't he have a fine head and face? Taken by Wilson Moore. Ten-year-old Mary C. Bet she was an exceptional baby, fat and pretty. Goes to C. H. Hawkins. Joseph P. Six years old, still speaks a little of that funny Irish language. Goes to Mrs. L. M. Leggett.' It was like musical chairs in reverse—one by one a child was taken away, leaving an empty chair behind.

"'Our next little lady,' the mayor said. 'It says here that she comes from a fine American family.'

"Lillian stepped to center stage into the circle of light and felt warmth wash over her. When she looked down at her arms, she almost didn't recognize them. She couldn't stop admiring how the spotlight gave her skin a milky glow like that of a marble statue.

"'An orphan like the others,' the mayor continued. 'But different from the others on the mother's side. This girl comes with a fine American pedigree, only her mother fell out of the good graces of her respectable family by a foolish act. I think you all know the kind of act I'm talking about without having to embarrass the ladies in attendance today. Under other circumstances, this girl would have been raised in the lap of luxury.'

"Now this was news to Lillian. What had been her mother's foolish act? And what was this *lap*? Lillian had never met anyone named Luxury. How could she have almost been raised in Luxury's lap?

"Lillian's thoughts were cut off by the sound of a woman's sharp, accusing voice ringing out from the audience: 'Pettygree or no pettygree. She sank her chomps into Tankersley.' Another voice hollered, 'Didn't offer no apology!'

"The mayor gave a fake laugh. 'All the more reason to open your hearts, folks.'

"But other voices drowned him out:

"*Incorrigible! Naughty! Shameful! Disrespectful!*

"*New York City manners! Should be locked up for what she done!*

"*Lock her up! Send her back!*

"With all the commotion, Lillian realized that she had to do something or she would be sent back to New York. Isn't that what the agent had told her? What could she do to redeem herself? How could she win them over, convince them that she was a special girl, a girl with vows and a future?

"The solution came to her. She walked over to the mayor, pulled on his shirtsleeve, and whispered something in his ear.

"'Folks! Folks! Listen here!' The mayor managed to get their attention. 'The little lady knows she did wrong, and she wants to make amends. She tells me that she's very good at singing and wants to provide a little entertainment.'

"He nodded in her direction. She walked to center stage. The audience grew quiet. Miss Charlotte Fry's neck strained forward. Lillian was nervous, all right. What if she forgot the words? What if they didn't like her? But then, her own past gave her all the encouragement she needed. The footlights and the velvet curtain reminded her of all the applause she had gotten on the streets of New York. Hadn't those people adored her! Aren't people all the same, New York or Nebraska? Won't these people love her, too?

"Her confidence swelled, and she began singing. She really gave it her all. Only this was not one of those nice hymns from church that Nebraska family people appreciate. It was a song that Lillian had learned on the streets—something lively and catchy about sailors and a woman who wears fancy underwear. Definitely not a song for a proper young lady.

"She did a dance, too, some fast-moving foot shuffling and twirling, and right before she got to the end, she swiveled her hips like a hoochy-coochy girl. When she curtsied, tiny droplets of sweat twinkled on the dark hairs of her arms. The shocked audience stared as if she had cast a spell. She heard a sharp, disapproving inhale of one hundred breaths. A cough. She heard the rustling of stiff clothing.

"And then there was not even a peep. Lillian stood in the spotlight frozen, like a girl in a field listening for a storm cloud to break. The only thunder was one pair of hands that started clapping and one voice, loud and thick with blueberry wine, saying, '*Dang!* That's good entertainment!'"

CHAPTER 25

"Hoochy-coochy girl!" Whitney imitated.

"She didn't go live with that Mr. Tankersley, did she?" I asked.

Fern asked Whitney, "What's a hoochy-coochy girl?"

Monica was chewing her nails. "I can't stand it if she went with that guy."

Fern again: "What guy?"

I repeated: "Tell me she didn't go with him."

"Oh, that guy!" Fern remembered.

"She did g-go. The committee routinely approved every single match, and Lillian didn't put up a fuss."

I couldn't believe it. Even Lillian, who would never fuss for no reason, wouldn't stand for this. "Why would she do that? What about her vows?"

Whitney was shaking her head sadly at me. "Man-oh-man, you think you know everything, but you don't know about kids like Lillian, kids like us."

"Why should I?" I sniffed. "I'm not really like you. My mother is—"

The Knitting Lady, who does not usually interrupt,

broke in. "Whitney, Cal is still new here. Tell her why Lillian would go with Mr. Tankersley."

"Let her figure it out herself!"

"A-Amber, can you explain?"

She began, "Where else could she—" Then Whitney couldn't stop herself, "Man-oh-man, Cal. Don't you get it? No one else wanted her even though she's the best kid in the bunch."

"Definitely the best," I said.

We agreed on that. Still, I was confused. Lillian had the guts to sing in front of an audience full of strangers. Lillian wasn't the type to be pushed around. So why would she go with smelly old Tankersley? There must have been plenty of other choices. There had to be. I explained my reasoning. "Lillian could have said to Miss Charlotte Fry, 'Excuse me, but I would rather go back home—'"

Whitney made an exceedingly rude raspberry sound. "What planet are you on? No one is waiting for her all lovey-dovey, 'Come home to me, precious baby jewel.' Face it, she's caught between a . . . a . . . Amber! What's she caught between?"

"A rock and a hard place," Amber answered.

Monica was explaining the latest turn in the story to Fern, who, as usual, was a few steps behind. "Lillian had so much courage! I would have been terrified to be up on that stage singing. Terrified! But not her."

"Yeah," Fern added. "She wasn't scared of anything. But she still had no other choice!"

"Right! Even Fern gets it," Whitney said. "Lillian's in the same boat as Basket Boy when someone came along and plucked him out of the reeds. What could he say? 'No thank you because I don't like the looks of you'?"

The Knitting Lady looked pleased. "Girls, I could not have put that better myself! Of course Lillian wasn't exactly weak in the knees with gratitude. But she knew she could handle whatever came. She reminded herself that she still had her vows in place. Going home with Mr. Tankersley wasn't a long-term thing. That's what she told herself. It was only a temporary stop on her way to her spectacular life."

When the Knitting Lady put it that way, it made sense to me. "Now I understand. Lillian didn't fuss because she knew this wasn't her real life."

"Th-that's exactly what she told herself, Cal. But this is as much a part of her story as anything else. It shaped who she was and what she would someday be. Lillian was too young to understand that yet. But everyone is always living her story."

So that's when she said it: *Everyone is always living her story.* And that's when I thought: *What kind of nutty philosophy is that? Who would buy it? Everyone? Always? Maybe Whitney and Amber belong here and maybe this is*

Monica and Fern's story, but not mine. But I let that particular subject drop and asked, "So, what happened next?"

The Knitting Lady raised an eyebrow.

"I know! I know!" Fern said, waving her arm in the air.

Of course, none of us could believe it. "*You* know?" Whitney asked suspiciously.

"Go on," Monica pressed.

Fern had a pleased look on her face. "What happens next is . . . we need to wait for another time."

"Exactly," the Knitting Lady said.

ை

That night before lights-out, Amber pulled out something from the top drawer in her dresser. It was one of those black-and-white notebooks that looks like it could start mooing any minute.

"What's that for?" I asked.

Amber opened to the first page and, in her pretty handwriting, wrote: *Life in the Pumpkin House. The main characters—Whitney, Cal, Amber.* Then she passed the book and a pen to Whitney.

"What do you want me to do? Nah-uh. I hate writing. This isn't school."

Amber took back the book and wrote: *But you have to. It's our story! We have to write it down.*

"Man-oh-man, okay, but only because I have to." She wrote: So what the heck am I supposed to write about? When she passed the book to me, I noticed that her penmanship was a lot like her knitting. As for my handwriting, it wasn't as pretty as Amber's, but more straight up and down. Teachers were always complimenting me because it's so easy to read. I wrote:

Mr. Tankersley gives me the creeps.

Whitney, did the Opera House remind you of something?

"What?" Whitney asked, then remembered that she was supposed to write. What??????

The Foster Kid Fashion Show.

"Yes!!!!! Man-oh-man, Amber, you're so right!" she said. "Makes me wanna barf just thinking about it. At least Lillian didn't have to keep changing into stupid clothes. They made me wear this stupid dress." In the book, Whitney wrote: Drawing of me in stupid dress

What's the Foster Kid Fashion Show?

Get down on your knees and pray that you never, ever have to be in one of those!!!! Whitney looked up from the book and said, "The time they made me be in it, I messed it up big time, so they never asked me again. If you do have to do it, make sure you mess up." She wrote: Fashion Show Advice—

173

Spill something or trip, then said, "The whole thing is so embarrassing, you'll want to crawl in a hole and die. You know it must be embarrassing because I'm not the embarrassed type."

But what is it???

I told you already!!! A fashion show!!!

???

A fashion show for kids who need foster homes or to be adopted.

They invite all the grown-ups who are thinking about adopting or taking in a foster kid. And then, they dress you in clothes that stores donate and you have to walk across a stage while everyone's watching.

I wouldn't like that! Cal Lavender doesn't like anyone staring at her!

They make you do it! It really sucks because you have a name tag and after the fashion show people who like the way you look come up and ask all sorts of personal questions. They pretend they're only making nice conversation, but you know their trying to decide whether they want to adopt you or someone else.

They're trying. It's not their trying. What kind of questions?

Like Whitney, how long have you been a foster kid? And Whitney, ha-ha, why are you so petite? That's the polite word for shrimp.

Then what happened?

I would have gotten adopted if I wanted to but people just pissed me off so I showed them my scar and that was that.

Some kids get new homes and some kids don't.

"That's unfair!" I blurted out. Then remembered to write, *That's unfair.*

"Amber's right," Whitney said. "We better write this stuff down so people will know our story." She wrote: End of Part One of the hysterical document by Whitney, Amber and Cal.

"Historical document," I corrected.

"Well, somebody better get hysterical over it!" Then Whitney slammed the cow notebook closed and stuffed it under her mattress. After that, she curled up around Ike Eisenhower the Fifth's home, like he was a real pet instead of a bug in a mayonnaise bottle.

I tried to sleep, but my mind kept spinning. *I won't be in a fashion show! I won't! And I wouldn't let Tankersley look at my teeth either!*

"Cal?" It was Amber. "Are you asleep yet?"

"Not yet," I said.

"Don't worry, Cal. I won't fall asleep. Not until you and Whitney do."

CHAPTER 26

Most average eleven-year-olds don't think very much about time. Unlike me, they haven't turned it around and around in their head and come to a very interesting conclusion: Time is strange. By this I mean that time can go both slow and fast at the *very same time.* Here's some examples:

Sometimes in the morning at the Pumpkin House, I would wake up groggy and reach for the familiar length of Betty's arm, and when I didn't feel it, I bolted upright. *Bam!* Time stopped.

Or at the most ordinary moments—like while I was brushing my teeth or knitting a row—Betty's face would materialize before me, hovering like one of those huge Thanksgiving Day parade balloons. *Now! Now! Now! I want Betty now!* At those moments, every second seemed like an hour. It was about three million times worse than sitting in class waiting for the bell to ring.

But time also had a way of flying by. I had to admit that, for not being my real life, things could sometimes get somewhat interesting around the Pumpkin House. For instance, one afternoon we went to the branch library, where I took it upon myself to introduce everyone to the Dewey decimal system. Personally, I don't know how anyone gets along without knowing the Dewey decimal system.

We also went to the park a lot, so much so that I began to think of it as Pumpkin House Park. I borrowed a bathing suit from Fern (same size as me), and we all went to the pool, even Monica who had to sit on a chair because of her arm cast. I didn't think she minded at all, because I assumed she was afraid of the water. She and the Knitting Lady sat together and laughed a lot.

The pool was as good as Whitney said it would be. There was a high dive *and* a big, mushroom-shaped canopy that sprayed water and made everyone screech. As anyone who knows Cal Lavender would suspect, I passed the swimming test the first time out.

One time, I was sitting out with Monica, and we were watching people go off the high dive. We watched one girl in particular. She was about fifteen and wearing a red one-piece with straps that crossed in the back. She paused a moment, then stretched her arms above her head. With a bounce, she dove, then she turned into a ball and spun in the air. Her body unfolded and became a straight arrow entering the water.

I was thinking that someday, somehow, I was going to know how to do that. But it surprised me when Monica—

always-scared-of-something Monica—said, "I want to know how that feels."

That was the first day that I really talked to Monica, and I learned all sorts of stuff that I never expected. We talked about things we wanted to do in life, and what seemed too scary and what seemed impossible. It was like discovering a whole new Monica! When the Knitting Lady said it was time to go home, it was already four o'clock. See? That's what I mean by time being weird and just racing by.

On Mondays, Wednesdays, and Fridays, it was my turn not to fall asleep until Amber and Whitney did. The other nights I got to fall asleep easier, just knowing that Amber was still awake.

One of the best times was the day we all went shopping. At first, I insisted that I didn't need any new clothes, since Betty was coming for me any minute. So why get things that I didn't need?

"I can just keep washing out what I've been wearing," I insisted.

But Whitney held her nose, and if Whitney was holding her nose, I realized I must be getting pretty ripe—and Cal Lavender is not the type of person who walks around being ripe—so I agreed to go. But just this once.

As I mentioned before, I was used to doing all my shopping at Sacred Heart Community Center where an eleven-year-old girl can walk in and pick out any kind of outfit she wants and it doesn't cost her one red cent. But the Knitting Lady insisted that it was time for me to have some-thing brand-new. "J-just for you," she said. "Something that hasn't been worn by anyone else. You deserve that."

I left the store with new red sneakers and a blue ging-ham two-piece bathing suit (my first two-piece) and a pair of pajamas that I really didn't need but the Knitting Lady insisted that I get because I had never before seen pajamas with a *One Fish, Two Fish, Red Fish, Blue Fish* design. I know I read at an eighth-grade level, so that particular book is way too young for me. But it's fun to have things that remind you of when you were in first grade.

I also saw time passing in other ways, like the way my knitting kept growing and growing until it tumbled to the floor, all yellow and gold, like Rapunzel's hair. I had made up my mind that if I couldn't be the most interesting knit-ter like Amber or the fastest like Whitney, I would be the longest knitter. Soon, I was working on what the Knitting Lady dubbed The Longest Piece of Knitting That Has Ever Been Knitted at the Pumpkin House.

I noticed time passing in Amber's hair, too. She had stopped pulling at it so much, and now eyelashes were beginning to sprout on her lids and the bald patches on her scalp were slowly filling in. It had been a long time since Fern's eye was swollen. You couldn't even tell that it had ever been bruised. And then one day, Monica went to the doctor to get her cast off, and, believe it or not, she didn't cry or even act scared. She came out of the doctor's office with a big smile and an arm that was pathetic-looking, white and so much bonier than the rest of her. She seemed to be getting braver about other things, too. She actually tried one of my Infinitely Superior Lettuce, Tomato, Cucumber, Avocado, Mustard, and Mayonnaise Tortilla Roll-Ups.

We worked on our Cow Notebook historical document almost every day, and I saw time passing in the way the pages were filling up.

Monica says I don't have the guts to go find my sister. Ha! Monica the wimp saying I don't have guts! You have to plan something like this. I've been planning my head off.

Picture of me planning my head off $\longrightarrow$

Monica's not such a wimp any-more. Anyway, there's no need to rush. You want to do this right, right?

Man-oh-man, we'd be gone by now if it wasn't for a certain something that I'm waiting for that's holding me back. Don't ask me what it is.

What is it?

Three guesses

The Knitting Lady's story. You don't want to leave before it's over.

Everyone would kill me if we left before the end, right?

Definitely! And who knows how long the story will go on?

What I didn't write was that I was hoping the story would go on forever. Or at least until Betty did whatever she had to do so that I could go back to my real life again.

∽

The next time I met with the social worker, I told her that I had been thinking very seriously about these so-called rules that Betty had to follow.

"Just what are these rules?" I asked.

Mrs. S. said it was very simple. There was just one rule really. Betty had to show that she was capable of taking care of me. "Instead of vice versa. You're the child and your mother is the adult. But you're the one who keeps taking care of her."

I thought: *What's the big deal? We get along fine— just fine—with me doing most of the taking-care-of. Rules are made for an average, ordinary family, but that's not us.*

I said, "Eleven and one month—no, two months now—is almost an adult."

Mrs. S. said, "Don't you believe it. Your mother has to start being the mother."

"But she's not like other mothers. How do you expect her to do that?"

Without looking up from my paperwork, the social worker said, "If your mother really loves you, she'll find a way to change and do what she's supposed to do. That's what a mother does."

"And if she doesn't?"

Mrs. S. didn't answer my question. But in the silence, I heard her answer: *It means she doesn't love you enough.*

∽

I tried to fall asleep that night, but couldn't. I needed an answer. I went looking for the Knitting Lady and found her in her bedroom.

"I have a for-instance question," I said.

The Knitting Lady yawned. "Don't mind my yawn. That's just age speaking. I'm always ready for a for-instance question. It gives the brain a chance to stretch. Go."

"Let's say that someone really wants to do something. It's a very important thing to do, and in their heart they want to do it. This thing that they want to do doesn't seem like a big deal. I mean, if you look around, you see that most people in the world have no trouble doing it. But for some reason, it's just hard for this person to do this thing because they're not the typical, average person and things that are no sweat for other people are really, really hard for them."

I paused to catch my breath and thought: *I'm making no sense at all.* I asked, "Am I making any sense at all?"

"Perfect sense. G-go on."

"I don't know what else to say. I just want to know if the person can do it or not."

"It depends."

"On what?" I felt my heart beating. "It depends on love, doesn't it? If the person loves enough, nothing will hold her back. And if she doesn't love enough, then she won't do what she should be doing. That's it, isn't it?" My voice got louder. "Isn't it?"

"Who said it's only a m-matter of love? Life is more complicated than that. For instance, Lillian's mother loved her, right? She loved her enough to give up everything. But love couldn't stop her from dying."

I shivered. "She left Lillian all alone."

"That's the way it seemed," the Knitting Lady said. "But that's because Lillian didn't know her own h-history."

"What history? She has no history! Her own family gave her away."

"That's not the h-history I'm talking about."

My words came out sharp and frustrated. "You keep talking about this history, how Lillian's a part of it, and Whitney and Amber, and me, too. But I don't know what you're getting at. I don't care. I just want Betty. If she loves me, she'll find a way."

I expected the Knitting Lady to launch into one of her

philosophical discussions, to go on and on about ancestors and things that I didn't want to hear about. I wouldn't listen to that! I waited for her to say the exact wrong thing so I could storm out of the room. She filled her mouth with air, and, for a second, I saw her skin the way it must have looked once, without the wrinkles of time. Then she blew out the air. There was a long, odd silence. She said nothing, nothing at all.

CHAPTER 27

First thing in the morning, the Knitting Lady called an emergency storytelling session. How can a story be an emergency? I pulled off my pajamas, folded them extra neatly, put on shorts and a top, then walked calmly down the stairs like I wasn't burning with curiosity, which I was, but Cal Lavender isn't about to let anyone know that she's burning with anything.

Whitney, of course, had no such restraint. She nearly pushed me over in her rush to get down. Monica and Fern were already in Talk Central, drowning their cornflakes in milk. Amber was in an armchair, her feet tucked under her bottom. She was knitting one of her creations with multi-colored yarn. Whitney flopped on the floor by my chair and, without asking, used my lap as a resting place for her stinky feet.

"If you don't mind," I said, lifting them and setting them back on the floor.

"What's the matter with you?"

I thought: *Why, nothing. Everything is just dandy. I've got a social worker who won't tell me about my own life, and Betty, who may or may not decide to become a mother—whatever that means, and where is Betty? And what happens if someone like smelly Tankersley decides that Cal Lavender is the exact type of girl he wants to take home? And please, please, please let Whitney forget about her plan to find her sister.*

"Nothing," I said. "Nothing is the matter. Everything is just great."

"Good!" Whitney said. "Because it's important that nothing's the matter with you. Because . . . you never know when big things may be happening. Big!"

I tried to avoid eye contact, but Whitney was bobbing all over the place, making sure that I couldn't escape her winking.

It was a big relief when the Knitting Lady put her finger to her lips, signaling us to be quiet. As far as I could tell, an emergency storytelling session was pretty much like a regular storytelling session, except that she started right in, no catching up or anything.

"L-Lillian was standing in the front yard of the Tankersley farmhouse. To a girl from a city, it all looked unreal, like a set in a snow globe before someone shakes it. In her mind, Lillian went over the things Mr. Tankersley had told her during the long, bumpy carriage ride: In the winter, they will get snow, plenty of it. Lillian will have her own room behind the alcove. Mrs. Tankersley has a sickness. Mr. Tankersley will teach Lillian how to candle an egg. Mrs. Tankersley has been sick for a while. Their closest neighbor is five miles away.

"Mr. Tankersley led her into the house. The front door squeaked and closed behind them with a slam. 'Let's go meet your new mother,' he said. 'But don't go making her laugh right away. It might set her heart palpitating.'

"When he opened the door to the dark bedroom, Lillian was hit with a closed-in smell, like the odor that rises from old water in a vase of rotting flowers. 'Ida,' he said. Then Mr. Tankersley made a big production of opening the curtains and shutters. When the light poured in, Lillian saw a new look on his face, something she never expected. The look was full of hope. Ida—his wife, Lillian's new mother—was in the bed, a woman as pale as chalk. The sight of her made Lillian shiver, like a cold finger had just run up her spine. The woman's eyes were oversized, like she was seeing horrible things that nobody else could see.

"Mr. Tankersley sat in the chair beside the bed and took the woman's hand in his. 'Ida, I brought you someone.' He turned to Lillian, gestured at her with his chin. 'Go on, then. Say hello to your mother.'

"Lillian remained in the doorway, looking at the specter in white propped against a heavy wooden headboard. She said, 'Hello.'

"'Hello, *Mother*,' he prompted. 'Call her that. Say, *Hello, Mother*.'

"Lillian cleared her throat with a cough. *Mother*? Call her Mother? This woman wasn't *anything* like her mother. This wasn't her life. But she said it anyway, 'Hello. Mother.'

"Mr. Tankersley nodded in approval. He kept nodding as if his movements were catching and his wife would be energized by them. 'Isn't that nice, Ida? Your new little girl has come to say hello.'

"More silence. But Mr. Tankersley continued as if his wife had spoken right up and a whole other side of the conversation had taken place. 'Your little girl is here now, Ida. Now and every day.' He turned back to Lillian. 'Come on now, you. Kiss your mother. Go on, closer.'

"Lillian took two steps. 'I can't. I can't,' she said.

"'Sure you can. It is your own sweet, dear mother waiting here for you.'

"'I can't,' she repeated. But then she did. The skin tasted dry and bitter.

"'You wanna say something to our little girl, Ida. She's waiting.'

"Nothing."

At this part, Fern spoke up. She was totally confused. "So, who's the lady in bed?"

"Man-oh-man, something's nutty with her," Whitney said.

"I'm not nutty!" Fern protested.

"Not you! The mother. I think she's sad," Monica said.

"S-sad? N-nutty? Any other ideas?"

"I think . . ."

"G-go ahead, Amber."

"I think her own daughter died. Lillian is supposed to be her substitute daughter."

"Whose daughter?" Fern asked.

It turned out that Amber was right. The Tankersleys had had a daughter who died, and Mr. Tankersley thought that a new girl would snap his wife out of being depressed. At this point, we were all feeling a little sorry for the Tankersleys. How could you not get depressed when you had a cute little daughter and that daughter got sick and then died in your arms? I, for one, was even hoping that Mrs. Tankersley jumped right out of bed and hugged Lillian and Lillian hugged her back and they all lived together happily in the farmhouse. I think we all liked that idea.

But the next part of the story made us change our minds. Whitney especially. Whew! It took the Knitting Lady several minutes to calm her down. When she heard that the Tankersleys gave Lillian the same name as their dead daughter—Faith—Whitney slammed her palm on a table. "I hate that! Man-oh-man, in my fifth—no! my ninth—foster home the mother kept calling me 'Patty.' Do I look like a Patty? No!"

"Is Patty the same as Faith?" Fern asked.

"No! Patty was some little kid who died. I felt bad because little kids aren't supposed to die. But man-oh-man, I got sick and tired of being Patty. I didn't die. I was plenty alive. It was *Patty, Patty, Patty.* So I ran away."

I would have done the same. Absolutely. Cal Lavender would never allow herself to be called anything other than Cal Lavender. So it was confusing to me that Lillian didn't seem to mind at all or at least she didn't show it. The Knitting Lady explained that she let the Tankersleys call her Faith, but she never, ever stopped thinking of herself as Lillian.

"Why?" I asked.

"B-because Lillian decided this wasn't her real life, so let those people call her what they wanted to call her."

That was something that I could definitely under-stand. But the name was just the start of Lillian's prob-lems. Ida Tankersley never jumped out of bed and hugged her. The haunted look never disappeared from behind her eyes. Eventually, Mr. Tankersley lost hope, and, with it, he lost interest in Faith/Lillian. If the girl couldn't cure his wife, then, by golly, she was going to have to earn her keep. Faith/Lillian began taking on all the farmwife chores. She cooked the breakfast, did the cleaning, the laundry, prepared the dinner. She ended each day by giving Ida Tankersley's hair one hundred strokes of a brush.

Days, sometimes weeks went by, when Mr. Tankersley

said little more than a few words to her. *Do this! Get that job done by sundown!*

"No school for Lillian?" Monica asked.

"N-no school."

"No friends?" Fern asked.

"T-too much work for friends. Besides, they lived out in the middle of nowhere."

Whitney was still all worked up. "No cakes dripping with honey either. Or dresses made of . . . made of what, Amber?"

"Gingham," she answered.

"Yeah. Gingham! But was there butter to church?"

"Churn," I corrected.

"And quilts to make? Hell, yes. I bet it was Cleaning Madness around the clock. Enough chores to choke a . . . choke a what?"

"Choke a horse," Amber and I said together.

"Yeah, a horse," Whitney said.

Monica said, "I would pass out if I had to do all that work! Unfair!"

The Knitting Lady agreed. "Y-yes, unfair! But compared to some of the other children who had come west, Lillian had it only half bad. At least she had food to eat and a roof over her head."

It turned out that some of the so-called *nice* families had lied like a rug. Some children were taken to farms and worked half to death. If the children refused to work, or passed out from too much work, well, they didn't get anything to eat. Some were given only rags to wear, and some got hardly any food, even when they worked all day and into the night. In the worst situations, the children were treated worse than the farm animals.

"They were hit," Amber said softly.

"T-that's true. I know it's hard to hear something like that."

Monica put her hands over her ears. "I don't want to hear it."

"N-nobody likes to hear it, but it's important to remember. Some of those children were . . . *hit* is not a strong enough word. They were beaten. And not one of them—not the laziest or the most ornery—deserved it. Not one."

I couldn't stop myself from looking at Amber just then. I couldn't help but think about what I had read in her social-work file, how in some ways, Amber's life had been even sadder and more unfair than what was happening to Lillian. Amber caught me looking at her, but she didn't turn away. Her expression didn't change. I repeated the Knitting Lady's words: "Not one deserved it. Not one."

Monica and Fern had also gotten quiet, which made me wonder what was written in their files. I would probably never know exactly what brought them to the Pumpkin House. But I knew that bad things had happened to them, too.

Maybe the Knitting Lady could read minds as well as she could read stitches: "Now, Cal, don't you go feeling all s-sorry for these children. Don't start pitying them. No pity! Do you know why? Because the things that happen to us—the bad as well as the good—make us who and what we are."

At that, we had a million comments and questions.

So, what happened to the little girl who looked like a boy? Did she get a pony or not?

And the brother of the red-haired girl?

No, not the brother! I want to know about the red-haired girl!

And the girl who was exceptional.

Exceptional?

Baby Mary, fat and pretty.

"S-some were lucky, some weren't," the Knitting Lady said. "And each one of those children has a story as dramatic as Lillian's. But to tell them now, all at the same time? Whew, I'm afraid my storytelling ability isn't up to that task."

"So go on about Lillian," Whitney insisted.

The Knitting Lady told us that Lillian did have one farm chore that she actually liked. That was to candle the eggs. I didn't have a clue what that meant and neither did anyone else, so the Knitting Lady explained. In the old chicken-farm days, eggs were held up to a light to see if they were fertile or not fertile. Tankersley taught her how to turn the egg quickly to throw the yolk near the shell. She knew she had a fertile one when she spotted the blood vessels of the embryo fanning out like a huge red spider.

"Gross! Why would anyone like that job?" Monica asked.

"Any i-ideas?"

I had one: "Even though she knows this is not her real life, she tries to be the best in everything." I paused. The Knitting Lady nodded in encouragement. "I think Lillian made up her mind to become the best egg candler in the entire state of Nebraska. She may not be the most creative egg candler or the fastest egg candler, but she was the best all-around egg candler." I had more to say, but I ran out of breath.

"There was one more thing our Lillian excelled at," the Knitting Lady went on. "One day, she was cleaning out a shed and found an old typewriter. It was rusty and some of the keys didn't work, but she taught herself to type. Pretty soon, neighbors were bringing her things that needed typing up. Most often, they paid her in produce and livestock. Mr. Tankersley got quite a number of chickens that way. But sometimes, she was given cash and managed to squirrel away a bit before Tankersley took the bulk."

"She was saving up for something!" Monica said.

"Something important!" Fern added.

"E-even Lillian wasn't sure what she was saving for, but she saved and saved. One Saturday when she was in town doing errands, she came upon a poster in the window of the dry-goods store. A vaudeville show was coming to town, and to say that Lillian was excited is putting it mildly. Every cell in her body longed to see new things, glamorous things that she knew existed in the world. So the promise of a vaudeville show? To see performers all the way from New York and even Europe? There was no doubt where some of her life savings would go. Without telling Tankersley, Lillian bought a ticket and for weeks could think of nothing else."

The Knitting Lady shut her eyes, not squeezed tight all scrunchy, but softly like a curtain dropping. She placed one hand to her heart and rested it there. If you looked closely, you could see it moving up and down to her breathing. She was really digging deep this time. Nobody said anything. We all knew better than to rush the Knitting Lady while she was gathering up the threads of her story.

"The Opera House," she finally said. "The place where lives are changed.

CHAPTER 28

"The v-vaudeville show was everything Lillian had dreamed of, and more. There was Peg-Leg Bates, a man with a leg as wooden as a broom handle, who danced his heart out. A woman played a ukulele like it was on fire. A man ate lit matches like they were chewing gum. Lillian clapped and clapped until her hands were red and stinging.

"And now an act called 'Little Miss' was scheduled to close the show. The curtain opened to a stage that was still and empty. Lillian wasn't the only one to feel a flutter of disappointment. Where was the swelling music and the fabulous set? Where was the dramatic opening that grabbed your attention and held it like a vise grip?

"Just as everyone was getting restless, a girl walked into the center of a single spotlight. She was pretty enough, with golden curls to her shoulders and enormous, round blue eyes. Normally, vaudeville audiences couldn't get enough of children's acts. But after so many hours of excitement, the audience was expecting more than one girl in a fluffy pink tutu. After all, this was the act that would send them back to their dusty farms and ordinary lives for another year.

"A piano player made a few light tinkling notes. The girl rose on the balls of her feet and made short, mincing steps that carried her forward and backward. Her arms rose listlessly up and down from her sides. But it was more than her mediocre dance talent that was making the audience squirm in their seats. There was something about this girl that seemed unbearably sad beneath her smile, like she was carrying the weight of the world.

"This was not what the audience had come to the theater to see! They wanted to escape the troubles of the world, not see them written on the face of an untalented child. You could hear their opinion of Little Miss in the whispers that traveled along the rows of the theater like a game of Whisper Down the Lane. *She's not a talented miss. Sad little thing. Sad little miss.* The pianist tried to add a little pizzazz with a quick, light running scale of notes. But Little Miss remained stilted and worn. She ended her act with a weak curtsy. Her hand went to her mouth, and she blew meaningless kisses.

"There was a clap here and a clap there, but the audience couldn't wait to get out of the theater. I'm sure that many of those people were thinking, *Tsk, tsk, such a young child should be going home with a proper family, rather than embarrassing herself on stage all hours of the day and night.*

"Suddenly, from the back row, came a man's voice that

reverberated throughout the theater: 'It's Nellie! Nellie! Don't you know me?'

"Everything came to a stop. Antsy kids who had fled into the aisles looked like they were playing a game of Statues. Wives paused midsentence, their mouths in perfect circles of astonishment. Husbands pivoted in the direction of the man's voice, their free hands set on their foreheads like sailors trying to spot land.

"Still nothing moved, except the man, his face thin and pale with emotion. He stretched out both arms and declared, 'I saw her picture on the posters! I've been tracking her from town to town. Nothing will keep me from her.'

"On stage, Little Miss, hearing the man's cry, froze with one hand in the air where her kisses sat half blown away. She peered across the footlights and then came alive. 'Poppa! Poppa! You came back for me like you said you would. Poppa, take me home!'

"What a commotion! The father rushed forward like a madman. Halfway to the stage, three confused ushers put their shoulders together to block his path. Still, he managed to push through the trio of burly, red-faced men. That was the strength of this skinny father's will!

"Next, the theater company manager—Mr. H. W. Mergenthal himself!—came onto the stage, shaking his fist. His features were hard, his voice all business. 'This is an outrage!' he bellowed. 'We don't know this man. Who is he?'

"'*She* knows me!' the father shouted.

"With a squeal of 'My poppa!' Little Miss took a step closer, but the piano player jumped up, scooped her into his arms, and carried her offstage.

"'She's our little star!' the company manager insisted, his voice coarse and threatening. 'She's under contract to us.'

"The father shook off the ushers like they were nothing but flies. He challenged the manager: 'What contract is more important than the bond between child and parent?'

"In the audience, the farmers and shopkeepers, the women and children rose from their seats, all of one mind:

"'Give him his daughter! Let her have her father!'

"'No!' H. W. Mergenthal shouted.

"'Yes!' the audience demanded.

"Mayor Clyde Shook pushed his way to the front. Wrapping a thick arm around the father, the mayor, his voice thick with outrage, said, 'I've never seen this man in my life. But he deserves to have his own flesh and blood. What's right is right!'

"At that, H. W. Mergenthal's chin dropped to his chest, and, when he looked back up, the hardness had slid off his features. His voice had a choke in it. 'I am so ashamed. Greed got ahold of me. But you fine, honest townspeople have shown me the light. Business can never come before family. Nobody can stand in the way of parent and child.'

"The piano player returned hand in hand with Little Miss, and, oh, what a difference! Her smile dazzled way to the back of the balcony. And what a dance she performed! A dance of gratitude. Her final dance. She spun and soared. She was air itself. And when she was done, to the cheers of the audience, H. W. Mergenthal lifted her in his arms.

"And what of our Lillian? She was transfixed. From the moment Little Miss had cried out 'Poppa!' Lillian had barely moved a muscle. Her mind latched on to an idea. No, it was more than an idea; it was the culmination of all her vows, of what she knew to be her destiny. Barely able to breathe, she watched as the manager stepped to the edge of the stage and handed Little Miss—a vision in pink-and-white tulle—to the father she always knew would come. At that, Lillian gave a low, involuntary cry of recognition.

∽

"Sh-she knew what she had to do. That night, when the Tankersleys fell asleep, Lillian packed her belongings. She didn't take much, some clothes, a hat she always liked. Right, Amber. Your fingers are in two circles. Of course, she took the lorgnette.

"She loaded the carriage and started driving to the

city. It was a good thing there was a full moon because the road was normally pitch-black and full of shadows that warn a young girl: *Turn around and go home!* But that night, there was plenty of light for Lillian to say good-bye:

"*Good-bye to dusty roads that lead nowhere.*

"*Good-bye to cows that stare dumbly behind the fence.*

"*Good-bye to thick air that turns everyone old and wrinkled.*

Good-bye to people who never really knew me.

"Lillian took one more thing—her typewriter. She wasn't sure why. It was a heavy, clunky old thing, but she trusted her instincts and threw it into the wagon at the last minute."

Monica looked worried. "Wasn't she scared?"

"Of c-course. Nobody heads into a whole new future without being scared."

I had a thought: "But Lillian told herself that she wasn't scared, not one little bit. Everything was going to work out."

"Well, did it?" Fern asked me.

"How should I know? It's not my story." I asked the Knitting Lady, "So did it?"

"W-work out? Mull that question over for a while, all of you. Next time, I want to hear what you think."

CHAPTER 29

I, Cal Lavender, have something to say about moods.

Most ordinary eleven-year-old girls are mood facto-ries, pumping out temper tantrums and hissy fits twenty-four hours a day. But not me. I don't have crying spells that come out of nowhere. I highly recommend this way of living because, from what I've observed, moods make you say and do enormously stupid things.

To tell the truth, grown-ups aren't always much better than kids. Mrs. S., the social worker, is a prime example. Someone with such an important job should not go from zero to a hundred on the ticked-off scale because of a few suggestions that I made at our next meeting:

SUGGESTION 1: Let's say, one sister is in a foster home and another sister is adopted. Shouldn't someone arrange things so those two sisters get to meet each other sometime?

SUGGESTION 2: Wouldn't it make her social-working job easier if Betty also lived in the Pumpkin House where I could help her do whatever it is she needs to do in order to pass the good-parent test?

These perfectly logical suggestions caused Mrs. S. to bristle. There were little drops of dried, white spit on the corners of her mouth, and they came flying off. "*Betty* has to cooperate," she insisted. "*Betty* has to put *your* needs before *her* needs."

What also surprised me was that the Knitting Lady could have moods, too. Sometimes, she would get flustered if she thought we were missing something important in her story. Once she got all weepy-eyed at something I said, but I'm not going to say what that was right now. Another time, I heard her go off like a siren—*Ooooooooh!*—when someone at the Department of Children's Services suggested moving Fern to a different group home for no real reason.

You would think that someone who had a finely developed knitting peace of mind wouldn't have moods. You would think! So that got me to reconsider my position. Maybe a mood or two isn't a terrible thing to have every once in a while. Maybe.

෴

Man-oh-man, Cal, I can't believe you told Mrs. S. that she should help me find my sister.

I didn't name names. I didn't say Whitney's sister!

U think you know everything but you don't know how everyone knows everything about U here. It's like they're part dog's nose. U even <u>think</u> something against the rules and Mrs. S. gets wind of it! Man-oh-man, I know she will. You screwed things up!

I didn't screw anything up!

I had another dream.

About my sister? Yeah it had to be! What????

She wants Cal to help find her. It won't work without Cal.

Says who??

Amber's dream! See, I didn't screw things up!

You did! But don't blow a gasnet about it!

A gasnet?

A gasnet! A thing on a car that blows up.

??????

A gasket. It blows up when a car gets too hot.

I'm not too hot! Cal Lavender is never too hot!

Hahahahahahahahahaha you're hot now. Cal is gasket hot!

That was when Whitney decided that we should have a test run before we really set off to find her sister. Considering it was Whitney's idea, it actually made sense. That night, we would wait until dark. Then, we would all climb out the window by my bed. I would check out the buses and map out a plan.

That's how I had things figured. If I went with them on the test run, they wouldn't need me when it came time for the real thing. Dream or no dream, I wouldn't have to go. I could stay in the Pumpkin House and be there when

Betty came to pick me up. That was my vow. I'd be back from the test run before anyone noticed we were gone. It was just practice.

∽

One more thing. Here's what I said to the Knitting Lady the time she got all moody weepy-eyed. "I have Betty's eyebrows," I was telling her.

"They're nice, s-strong brows."

"Do people always get things from their mother?" I hesitated. "Like a stutter?" I had never asked about her stutter, but she didn't seem to mind at all.

"My mother didn't stutter, if that's what you're asking."

"I keep watching out for them," I said.

"For what?"

"For Betty's moods. If I have her eyebrows, one day I could have her moods, too."

"You w-worry about that?"

"They could sneak up on me. Sometimes . . ." I paused.

"Go on."

"Sometimes I wish I *would* get Betty's moods. Inherit them. All of them!"

"W-why on earth?"

"Because then I'd know."

"Know what?"

"Exactly how Betty feels."

That's when the Knitting Lady got the weepy look.

Anyway, that's all that I, Cal Lavender, have to say about moods for right now.

CHAPTER 30

The big night. As I mentioned before, it was Whitney's bright idea to make our getaway through the window above my bed.

"No way," Monica said.

"Go!" Whitney ordered me.

"Go where?" I was staring two stories straight down onto a slab of hard, neck-breaking concrete patio.

"Just go! Jeez-Louise, I thought you said you'd climbed out windows before."

"I did. Lots of times. Sometimes Betty didn't pay the landlord and we had to—"

Whitney gave me a sharp push. "Go, then!"

"Usually, there was a fire escape. I assumed you were going to have a ladder."

Whitney spoke in a mocking baby voice. "'I assumed you'd have a ladder.'"

I faced her with my hands on my hips. "I hate people imitating me!"

Whitney threw herself, dirty shoes and all, on my bed. "I got another idea. I saw this in a movie once. Did you ever see that movie, these two firemen—no, it was three firemen, and maybe it wasn't a movie, maybe it was a TV show—well, they were stuck on the roof of this building— and you can't believe the flames—well, the girl in the movie, she—"

I broke in. "Are we going or not, Whitney?"

"Jeez, of course, I was getting to that. Anyway, the two firemen held the bravest fireman by the ankles out the window and lowered him—"

Monica looked pale. "I'm not doing that. No way I'm doing that."

"Did I see that movie?" Fern said. "Can we go to a movie tonight?"

Whitney ignored both of them. "As I was saying, Cal and Amber can hold me by my feet and lower me head- first to the ground." She picked up the mayonnaise jar.

"What are you doing with that?" Fern asked.

"You think I'm going anywhere without Ike Eisen- hower the Fifth?" She tapped on the side of the jar. "Don't worry, Ike. I won't go anywhere without you!"

She had to be kidding. I said, "You have to be kid- ding!"

What happened next was so logical and so practical that it was something I would definitely have thought of myself if Amber didn't get there first. "Come on," she said.

Her head was poking halfway into the hallway,

looking left, then right. She went first, then Fern and Whitney. Monica seemed paralyzed, so I pushed her ahead of me. And just like that, all five of us—six if you count Ike—went slinking down the stairs and across the living room floor. I made sure the door stayed unlatched when it closed behind us.

"Piece of cake," Whitney said.

Outside, a thick, warm mist was falling. It wasn't much of a rain, just enough to wet down the sidewalk and release the smells of concrete. "Let's go, let's go," Whitney urged, then turned and started walking up the street. No, it wasn't walking. She was more like a dog pulling on a leash. Right behind her was Amber, wearing clothes the same color as her skin, a pale gray, like the world never stopped raining on her. Next were Monica and Fern with their arms looped around each other's shoulders.

I thought: *Maybe the entire Department of Children's Services knows exactly what we're up to and right now they're deciding that I've blown any chance to ever go back with Betty. That's it! I am definitely going to turn around and go back into the Pumpkin House.*

That's what my logical brain decided. But my feet started doing a very un–Cal Lavender type of thing. I followed the others. I noticed a mockingbird on a telephone wire, whirring and clicking deep in its throat. And then I noticed the sudden cry of a cat, the whoosh of a car tire, the hum of a streetlight. I have to admit that I felt a charge from all these night sounds, like being with Betty when she was in one of her all-night moods. I was flooded with a sense of freedom, like I'd been suffocating and hadn't even realized it.

I thought: *Lillian must have felt this way when she left the Tankersleys in the middle of the night. The feeling of being the only one awake when other people are asleep. It must have felt just like this, like anything and everything was possible, like a whole new life was waiting for her just up the road.*

I hunched my shoulders against the drizzle and kept walking. Nobody would understand this feeling. Nobody but Lillian. Nobody but Betty. Nobody but me.

When I finally caught up with the others, they were clustered around the bus stop. Whitney was up and down from the bench, tapping on Ike Eisenhower the Fifth's jar, jiggling her right leg, popping four sticks of gum into her mouth at once. "Man-oh-man," she said.

That's when I saw something in her expression that was as familiar to me as if I had just run my hands up and down my own face. "What?" I asked.

"Man-oh-man, Cal. You know! The Pumpkin House is the best place I've ever been. But there's nothing—nothing!—like blowing out of a foster home."

I checked the posted schedule. The last bus on this

particular route came at ten p.m., so next time, Whitney would have to get an earlier start. "This is the number 26," I explained. "It'll take you downtown. Do you want to go downtown?" (Notice how I cleverly said "take *you*," not "take *us*.")

When she didn't answer, I went on. "That's where all the buses leave from. You'll have to know which one to catch after the 26. Do you know which bus goes to your sister's neighborhood?"

Whitney pulled out her wad of gum and stuck it to the bottom of the bench. Then, she started working on an open bag of sunflower seeds. *Crack.* "How could I"—*crack, crack*—"know which bus to take?" *Crack.* "You're the bus genius."

"So what's your sister's address?"

Whitney spit out a shell by her feet. "It's a secret! I had to steal to get it."

"I can't tell you what bus to take if I don't know where she lives."

Whitney glanced around, checking for her usual spies. "You'll know," she said, "when you need to know."

And that was that. That was the full and complete story of our practice run to find Whitney's sister.

CHAPTER 31

At 11 a.m. What a slug! I'd never slept that late before, not even when I was up all night with Betty.

At 11:05 a.m. Amber was still asleep. I peeked into the next room. Fern and Monica were still snoring away. What time did we finally come back in? Late.

At 11:15 a.m. At first I thought that maybe the Knitting Lady was also still asleep. That's how quiet it was downstairs. Then I heard mumbling coming from Talk Central.

I must point out that Cal Lavender never eavesdrops. Eavesdropping is something that a Whitney type of person would stoop to do. Eavesdropping is not polite at all, so I would never eavesdrop. That said, in this particular situation, I just happened to be standing behind the half-open door, waiting for a break in the conversation. The conversation that I wasn't eavesdropping on went like this:

K.L. (Knitting Lady): If you get s-some vows in place, you can have anything you aim for.

W. (Whitney): Like what?

K.L.: Well, some people aim for a big job and some people aim for a big car and some people want big adventures.

W.: What did you want when you were my age?

K.L.: I guess I wanted love. Love as big as a van.

W.: I want . . . I know what I want but I'm not telling.

K.L.: Fair enough. But to get it, you have to make a decision.

W.: What kind of decision?

K.L.: You can keep wanting what you don't have. Or you can open your eyes and start seeing what you c-can have, what you already have.

W. *(anger in her voice)*: Just because I'm a foster kid, I'm not gonna settle. That's what some of those orphan-train kids did! But not Lillian!

K.L.: No, not Lillian.

W. *(mocking voice)*: What am I supposed to say? Oh thank you, thank you, because I wasn't stuck on a train in 1892 and worked to death! Man-oh-man!

K.L.: Not what I'm saying. I w-would never suggest being grateful for that.

W. *(her voice softer now)*: Then what? What are you saying? What do I have?

There was silence. I moved a little closer to the door opening. I wanted to see what they were doing in the silence. What was the look on Whitney's face? What was the Knitting Lady doing? Was she talking about Whitney's sister? That was it! That must be it! Or was it something else? What *did* Whitney already have?

The Knitting Lady spoke again. "Cal? Come on in. Better yet, go upstairs and wake the others. What sleepy-heads! You'd think they were gallivanting about all night! I'm an old lady, you know, so I don't have forever to finish this story.

〜

"So, d-do you remember the question that I asked you to think about?"

Fern burst out, "I do! I remember! Did everything work out the way Lillian wanted it to?"

"G-good for you, Fern."

"See, I can remember things. I can."

"Who w-wants to take a stab at the answer? Monica?" She shook her head.

"C-Cal? Anyone?" She sighed. "No one. I guess you'll just have to wait and see.

〜

"From the front door of the Opera House, Lillian heard the grunts and pounding of men doing hard physical work. She hesitated. No! If she hesitated, she would never get what she wanted. So she stepped inside and looked around at the big men with paint and dust on their clothes and in their hair. One man was breaking apart the acrobats' trapeze. Two others strained to move a couch. Then, there he was!

"That early in the morning, H. W. Mergenthal certainly didn't look like the dazzling company manager of the night before. He held a clipboard, looking like a squat, tired, irritable middle-aged man. Lillian didn't want to lose her courage. So she carried all she owned in the world to the foot of the stage, dropped it by her ankles, and said, 'I'm here for the part.'

"One of the workers elbowed Mergenthal in the side. She heard him say, 'Wouldn't be a small town without at least one.'

"*Without at least one of what?* she wondered.

"The manager turned and took in everything about Lillian at once—her suitcase; her earnest, eager look; her cheap farm-girl clothes. 'So,' he said. 'You wanna join vaudeville.' His hands flipped up from the wrists like he was balancing two heavy trays. 'What's your act?'

"Lillian flashed him a smile that she had been rehearsing just for this moment: 'You are looking at Little Miss.'

"Mergenthal's lips tightened slightly like he just burped up something sour. 'Hey, kid, didn't you see the show? We have a Little Miss.'

" 'It must be a terrible blow, her going back to her father and all,' she said. 'But your troubles are over. I can replace her.'

"As Lillian was talking, she didn't see the creeping smile of amusement that came over the great man's face. She didn't notice how the workers started nudging one another. But she did notice when a woman, very short and small-boned with close-cropped dark hair, came onto the stage from the wings and called out, 'Harry! When are we out of here?'

"H. W. Mergenthal held up a warning finger to the woman and said her name sharply—'Florence'—before turning back to Lillian. 'What's your name, hon?'

" 'Lillian.'

" 'Okay, Lily. Just how old are you?'

"She lied. 'Seventeen.'

" 'Right,' he said, sarcastically. 'And I'm twenty-one.'

" 'Sixteen, then.'

"He paused like he was going to argue again, then changed his mind. 'Okay, sixteen-year-old Lily of Nebraska. First of all, let me introduce you to Little Miss.'

"The dark-haired woman named Florence rolled her eyes, and Lillian noticed they were blue. Very blue. And very round. H. W. Mergenthal noticed that Lillian noticed.

" 'Smart girl,' he said. 'Add a blond wig, the right makeup, and Florence can pass for fourteen, though she's a long way from that.' The woman gave him a light punch on his shoulder. 'It's all an act,' she explained flatly.

"Lillian repeated the words in her head: *An act. All an act.* Which meant that Little Miss had never really been taken from her family. Which meant that there really was no Little Miss. Which meant that . . . that . . . Lillian felt her future, her destiny, the very vows that had sustained her through those hard, cold Nebraska winters, begin to disintegrate around her. People would never know her name. Her life would never be spectacular.

"And there was something else. Something so important that Lillian did not even acknowledge it to herself. And don't say that you don't know. I know that each one of you knows."

Fern, of all people, began, "When she was watching Little Miss . . ." Monica continued, "Lillian thought that if her name was on a poster . . ." Whitney broke in, "And if she was famous and on stage . . ."

"Y-your turn, Amber."

"That someone would find her, too. Her father, maybe. Or one of those rich relatives."

"Understand, C-Cal? So what was it? What was that hope deep inside of Lillian?"

"That . . . that someone would rush to the front of the stage and take her back to her life, her real life. But Lillian didn't say that. She would never say that out loud!"

"Of c-course not! H. W. Mergenthal shrugged. 'Sorry, kid. We don't need a Little Miss.' He paused. He probably felt sorry for her. 'But you got spunk. There's always room for another spunky-kid act.'

"Lillian jumped on her second chance. 'I can sing,' she said, even though she had not sung in years.

"H. W. Mergenthal rubbed his cheek. 'Can't use another singer. How about spitting fire? A kid spitting fire would be something to see!' But when she shook her head, she noticed that the light in the man's eyes dimmed a little.

"*No!* she decided firmly. She can't get back in the carriage and return in shame and defeat to the Tankersley farm. Not when she had come this close—*this close!*—to fulfilling her vows. If the troupe would just take her along with them—take her to the next city and the next and the next—she would do anything. She didn't even have to be on stage. That was it! She could be useful in some other way. Think practical.

"H. W. Mergenthal started barking orders to the workers, moving upstage, downstage, stage left and right. When he got back to Lillian, he seemed surprised that she was still standing there. 'So . . . um, er, Lily, think of anything you can do?'

"'I can type,' she said. 'I'm the fastest typer you've ever seen.'"

"How fast?" Monica asked.

The Knitting Lady moved her fingers in imitation. "That's exactly what the theater manager wanted to know. At that point, Lillian could type fast enough to impress farmers, but it wasn't enough to suit the needs of the great H. W. Mergenthal. It would take Lillian hours and hours of practice to bring up her speed. She had to work on her accuracy, too. Typing and knitting have a lot in common. If you're fast but make a lot of mistakes, nobody has much use for that."

I shot a pointed look at Whitney, but she didn't seem to recognize the tie to her own particular knitting disasters. Rather, she was bombarding the Knitting Lady with opinions: "A few mistakes don't matter!" And, "Man-oh-man, she's not going to be a typer forever. Typing is too boring." And, "Skip typing and get to the next good part!"

The Knitting Lady got one of her knowing smiles. I imagine it was the same smile that the great H. W. Mergenthal got when he knew he had pulled a good one on the audience. "You w-wouldn't be saying that if you remembered."

Fern pounced. "What? Remember what? What?"

"Relax, Fern," Monica said. "No one remembers."

"I planted a h-hint, way back in the story."

We all turned to Amber, who had a blank look. Then, when everyone looked at me, I pointed out, "It couldn't have been a very good hint if not even Amber or I can remember. Maybe you need to plant your hints a little better."

"Cal, I w-will certainly take that suggestion to heart. Pulling all the pieces of a story together is not the easiest thing in the world, but I want to do my best. Let's forget the hint for now and go back to the theater. The workers put together a makeshift desk from some crates and placed Lillian's typewriter on top. She cracked her knuckles. 'What should I type?' she asked.

"Mergenthal flipped through his clipboard and pulled out a sheet filled with names, dates, and dollar amounts. 'See what you can do with this.'

"Her typewriter was an old Underwood model, the kind of machine you only see now in old movies. It must have weighed a ton and a half. And the noise! When Lillian started typing, you could hear that clickity-clackity-clack all the way to the balcony. H. W. Mergenthal circled Lillian, looking at her from every angle. Every once in a while, he snapped an order that she did her best to follow:

"'Straighten your back! No, not like someone just slapped you with a whip. More relaxed! Graceful. Sway a little.'

"'Make some fou-fou movements with your hands. And smile! Can't you smile?'

"Truthfully, the typing was taking so much of Lillian's concentration that she didn't even consider what she looked like. Besides, what did it matter if she was biting her lower lip and frowning so hard that a V formed between her eyebrows? Why on earth did she need to smile? But she straightened her back and smiled and swayed. She tried to imagine that she was playing a complicated piece of music on the piano instead of typing letters onto a cheap piece of white paper.

"'Good fou-fou,' Mergenthal said.

"Lillian thought: *He won't be saying that when he sees all the mistakes. He'll never hire me then.* She watched his face carefully as he ripped the paper from the roller and studied it with a lot of 'hmmmmm's' and 'uh-huh's.'

"'Gotta get faster,' he finally said. 'And can't have any mistakes. None! We'll aim for what? What sounds good— 99 percent? No, 99.9 percent accurate.'

"'I'll practice, sir, practice till my hands fall off—99.9 percent, sir!'

"Again, Mergenthal didn't comment. He kept looking at Lillian, and, without taking his eyes off her face, he yelled, 'Florence, bring your red case.'"

It was here that the Knitting Lady made an interesting comment. "Ten, eleven, twelve, thirteen are fascinating ages. One minute I can see the little girls you were, and the next I can see the women that you'll soon be. It doesn't take much. Just the trick of light hitting you one way or another."

I knew what the Knitting Lady was saying. For

example, Whitney looked one age in her body and another age in her face. Now that Amber's hair was growing back in, she didn't look like a sad little ten-year-old. I would have to say that she looked at least eleven."

"What about Lillian?" I asked. "Did she look older or younger than she was?"

"That's w-what I'm getting to. Inside the red case were the tools to make Lillian any age that they wanted her to be."

"Lipstick!" Whitney yelled. "Eye shadow, lip liner, eyeliner."

"The whole k-kit and caboodle. No Nebraska farm girl ever wore makeup, so Lillian didn't really know what was happening to her. The puffs of sweet-smelling p-powder on her skin and the feel of hands fussing with her hair, piling it into a great beehive on her head. When Florence was done, she stepped back to admire her work."

"I don't get it," Fern complained. "All that fuss to be some typing person?"

Amber said something softly, which the Knitting Lady asked her to repeat. "The Fastest Typer."

That was the big hint! I had one word in my mind so I said it: "Digits."

I knew the Knitting Lady heard me, but she had a far-away look. She was back in Nebraska with Lillian. "So, the great H. W. Mergenthal said, 'What do you think of this? Lovely Lily with her Delightfully Dexterous Digits.'"

"Oh!" Monica burst out. "I get it."

"Get what?" Fern shouted.

I wiggled my fingers, which made Whitney slap her palm on her forehead—"Oh!" Then, Fern also said, "Oh!" only I'm not sure if she really got it or just didn't want to feel left out.

"B-but Lillian shouted, 'No!' "

"What did she mean by *no*?" I asked.

"That's the same thing that H. W. Mergenthal asked. He was not a man used to having anyone say no to him.

"But Lillian stood her ground. She announced to everyone, 'No, not Lily. *Lillian. Lovely Lillian with her Delightfully Dexterous Digits!*' "

CHAPTER 32

Later that day, the Knitting Lady took us to the pool, which is one of the best places for avoiding conversations of a serious nature. Whitney kept trying to bring up her only topic—the search for her sister—but all I had to do was turn an underwater backward somersault or act like my ears were too clogged with water to hear a word. For a while, Whitney even distracted herself by insisting that we put our butts up against the warm-water jet to experience the magnificent sensation.

WHITNEY: It's just like one of those fancy Jack Uzi things. I'll bet my sister has one in her own personal bathtub.

FERN: One of what?

AMBER *(correcting)*: A Jacuzzi.

ME: *Performing dead man's float for forty-eight seconds, my all-time breath-holding record.*

MONICA: So when are we going to track her down? I'm not scared at all of going!

FERN: Going where?

MONICA: Fern!

FERN: Oh, going you know where.

MONICA: To find you know who.

FERN: Who?

ME: *Out of the pool, walking slowly to the deep end, cannonballing off the side.*

LIFEGUARD (*blowing whistle at me*): No diving off the sides!

Whitney and the others kept appearing inches from where I landed. Wherever I swam, there they were.

WHITNEY: I'm just waiting for her to finish the story and then we'll go.

ME: *Sitting on the bottom of the pool, legs crossed.*

When I came up for air, I was cornered, wedged between the steps and a semicircle of Pumpkin House girls. Whitney was saying, "She's near the end of the story!"

I said, "You don't know that."

She said, "Of course I do," and I came back with "How do you know?"

"Well . . . ," Whitney hesitated. "Amber, how do I know?"

"Because," Amber said, "that's the way a story works. It starts one place and circles back to the beginning."

"We're back to digits," Whitney said, and then demonstrated by turning a somersault in the water.

"I'm freezing," I said. "I need to get out."

I hoisted myself onto the edge of the pool and grabbed my towel. "Gotta pee," I said. They wouldn't follow me if I had to pee.

They followed me. They waited outside the stall. Then they crowded around the sink while I washed my hands. I said, "She could be tricking us and not be anywhere near done with the story."

Fern edged close to the mirror, inspecting her nose for blackheads. "Why would she trick us?"

"Because . . . ," I said. "Because . . ." *Because I don't want the Knitting Lady to be near the end of her story, because if she is, it means that Whitney is going to demand that I run off to find her sister, and while I think that's just fine for her to do, because this* is *her life, I'm not about to put* my *whole life at risk.*

I said, "Whitney, don't you need another test run?"

"Naw on test run. You can lead the way when we take off."

I looked in the mirror. My eyebrow was buckled in the middle. I flashed on my most recent conversation with the social worker, who told me that Betty was showing signs of—*quote*—coming along—*unquote.* Mrs. S. sounded surprised beyond belief. The next thing she said—*So you better stay put!*—returned to haunt me.

I lifted my soapy hands to my face, brought them down again. "Not really," I said.

Behind me, Whitney was talking to my reflection. "What's that mean?"

"Not really what?" Fern asked.

"Not really . . ." There was no way to tiptoe around this. "I'm not going with you."

Fern stopped squeezing blackheads. Monica backed away and collapsed onto a bench. Amber's hand dashed to her mouth, then dropped back to her side.

Whitney stuck her finger in her ear. "Man-oh-man, my ear must be clogged with pool water. I swear I didn't hear right."

"It's not like you actually need me to go. I'm perfectly willing to provide you with the most detailed bus information possible."

"You're not going?" Fern started giggling, then turned to everyone else—"She's not going?"—and then back to me— "How can you not be going?"

Whitney didn't leave me a chance to explain. "Because, she still thinks Betty is going to show up any minute and whisk her away back—"

"—to my real life," I said. "The social worker said I could be going home any time now."

"She did not!" Whitney insisted.

"She said something like it. She said— How do you know what she said or didn't say?"

"I listened in. She didn't say that!"

I swirled around. "I hate eavesdroppers."

Whitney didn't miss a beat: "Liars who say they are going to do something but then don't are the scum of the earth."

"I never said I'd go with you."

"Scum of the earth!"

And then Monica said that I should think about Whitney instead of always thinking about myself, and Fern said, "Yeah," and Whitney said, "Don't you get it, Cal? This *is* your real life. You're one of us. Family. Sort of, in a way, kind of."

Some family.

"Look at me," I said. "Do I look like I'm listening to what any of you are saying?"

I leaned over the sink and washed all the soap off my face.

⟡

Why do you need me? You said I don't know anything.

Not about life in here, but out there you, Cal Lavender, your a woman of the world. We need a gliding light!

It's you're, not your. And guiding. You mean a guiding light.

No, you can glide us through the city. Wait! Now I

know why you don't want to go! Your jealous I have a sister and you don't.

You've got to be kidding.

It's okay, Cal! Don't be embarrassed. I know how it feels, but don't worry. I won't let you down. I'll share. We'll all be sisters. She'll be your sister too.

They worked hard on me, but I told them over and over: No! Finally it got through. "End of discussion!"

For days after that, war was declared in the Pumpkin House, and I was the enemy. On the stairs, Whitney just *happened* to stumble and push me into the banister. They made sure I was the last one to the van and locked the door until the Knitting Lady insisted that they open it. Monica kept appearing out of nowhere and asking, "What's up *your* butt?" Fern laughed hysterically every time she saw me. Even Amber. Her eyes kept darting away from me like I was an enormous embarrassment.

Then things escalated.

Someone put shaving cream on my toothbrush. Someone dumped Rice Krispies on my bed. Someone wrote a note telling me to call Betty but when I called the number, I got Dial-A-Prayer. Someone unraveled six inches of my knitting.

Don't think for a minute that any of this bothered me.

∽

One day after lunch, I sneaked into the bedroom and slipped the Cow Notebook from under Whitney's mattress. I really didn't care what they were saying about me, but I figured I should see if Whitney was plotting anything dangerous. That was my right! I opened to the last page that had writing on it. It also happened to have Whitney's fingerprints in jam on the corners.

Hahahahahahahahaha! I knew it! I knew you'd look!

I slammed the book shut.

⟳

Then for days, no one tied my shoelaces together or threw my bathing suit out the window. No one made snotty remarks when we were in the grocery store or tried to trip me as I walked to the refrigerator. Whitney didn't stand over my juice, make a ball of spit, and let it drop in a long string into the glass.

They ignored me. I have to admit that they were exceptionally good at it. Your average, ordinary girls can't pull off the silent treatment for more than a day or two. Somebody eventually cracks. But they were better than most.

Don't think that any of this bothered me either.

⟳

After about four days into their stupid, silent grudge, I found myself feeling extremely strange. If Cal Lavender was a person prone to having moods, I would say that I woke up feeling sad and scared and angry and unhappy and lonely. For some reason, my eyes kept tearing up.

Maybe it was allergies.

I gathered up my knitting—congratulating myself once again on making the longest knitting project ever produced in the Pumpkin House even though certain jealous, petty people had unraveled some of it. I went downstairs.

Nobody but the Knitting Lady was around. Good. Everyone else was . . . I didn't care where they were.

The Knitting Lady took a quick look at me and stopped washing dishes. I followed her into Talk Central. "I'll stitch," I said. "But I have nothing to bitch about. Everything is just fine."

I knitted a row. The Knitting Lady finished her row, flipped her yarn, and started down the other side. She was humming—*hum, hum, hum*—I think it was one of those old-time songs that Lillian sang on the streets of New York.

This was better. I was definitely starting to feel less strange. I settled into my knitting. I was going home soon. Who cared about Whitney? Or Amber? Not me. Who cared if Monica or Fern ever talked to me again? Not Cal Lavender. I didn't care.

But then the stitches blurred up because my eyes were all full again. I set down the needles, gave them a little push. Half the length of my knitting tumbled to the floor.

"This is weird," I said.

The Knitting Lady handed me a tissue. I dabbed at the

puddles in the corner of my eyes. It was a good thing she didn't insist on having a heart-to-heart conversation because that was the last thing I wanted to have. She kept knitting and humming.

"I'm done with this," I said. I meant that I was done with the Kleenex. But as soon as I said it, I realized I was done with more than that. I was done with the teary eyes and feeling strange, with everyone and everything that had to do with the Pumpkin House.

"Done with your knitting?" she asked.

I was done with that, too. "It's long enough. Here!" I thrust the needles at her.

But she wouldn't take them. Rather, she bent with an old-lady groan and scooped up the section of my knitting that had fallen to the floor. "N-nice," she said. "But it's not finished yet."

"How will I know it's finished when I don't even know what it is?"

"Oh, d-don't worry about that. It'll be done when it's done. You can knit while I tell you more of the story. The others heard this part earlier this morning. You don't want them knowing something you don't know, right?"

I shook my head very quickly.

"That's very important. You girls all have to be on the same page. . . . Ready?"

I made one stitch and by the time I reached the end of the row, the Knitting Lady was bringing me up to date.

CHAPTER 33

No vaudeville performer ever put more effort into her act than Lillian did, the Knitting Lady told me. During the long train rides between cities, while waiting backstage during rehearsals, in lonely boardinghouses in the middle of the night, Lillian practiced.

To demonstrate, the Knitting Lady placed her needles at her side, sat up with exaggerated straight posture, and danced the pads of her fingers on her thighs. "Lillian drove herself mercilessly, like a great athlete trains," she said. "Day after day after day, no rest, no excuses until Lillian reached the world record. Twenty-five taps a second. *Thwack-thwack-thwack.* So fast that the sound came out as one long continuous *thwack.* And still, she kept practicing."

The Knitting Lady said that there were times when Lillian's head felt as though it would split like an egg from the intense concentration. Her hands sometimes cramped so badly that she couldn't even pick up a fork. But the physical pain was nothing compared to the voices in her head.

"You mean . . ." I made cuckoo circles by my temple.

"N-not *those* kinds of voices. The voices that say, *I can't. Someone like me—a kid who doesn't live with a mother and father—can't be the best. I can never make anything of myself.*"

"Lillian felt this way?"

"I know she did."

I disagreed. "I don't believe it. Lillian wasn't the type. She did everything so perfectly. Remember her vows? She was unstoppable. You said so in the story."

"An interesting p-point. But being unstoppable doesn't mean she had no doubts. It meant that she was willing to drive herself to perfection, to do anything to stem the flow of doubts. Do you understand?"

I hesitated. "I think . . . well, maybe it means that when Lillian was typing, she got all wrapped up in the typing like some people do when they're knitting or cleaning. She could forget everything else."

"L-like?"

"Like forgetting about her mother. And rich relatives who thought they were too good for her."

"All that. So you see that Lillian was two ways at once—both incredibly resourceful and independent. But also full of doubts and sadness—anger, too."

That was a confusing thought to me. "You mean she was living two different lives at the same time?"

The Knitting Lady closed her eyes in a that's-a-tough-question-to-answer kind of way. "I think you're asking something else."

"I am?"

"I think you're asking if Lillian ever got over losing her mother."

I felt those words deep in my ribs. "Did she?"

"No, she n-never forgot. But she eventually understood that accepting her new life didn't mean she was cheating on her old one. Do you know what I mean by that?"

I didn't, but in a way I did. I said, "Oh," because I couldn't think of anything else to say.

"Any m-more questions?" When I shook my head, she said, "Well, that's that. Now you're all up to date on the story."

༄

Whitney was the first to break the silent treatment.

I had gone over to the park by myself and saw them, a circle of my enemies around the teeter-totter, their backs to me, their heads bowed like they were praying. Then their heads bolted up, and Fern let loose with one of her nervous, high-pitched giggles. Whitney had a toothpick in her mouth. She moved it from one side to the other. "Oh, it's just *you*. I was scared it was *her*."

"Her who?"

"The Knitting Lady."

Monica looked at me suspiciously. "You didn't tell her anything, did you?"

"Of course not."

"Not that there's anything left to tell," Whitney said. And together, both Monica and Fern hissed in my direction, "Thanks to *you.*"

"Me? Why me?"

"Didn't you hear the big news?" Monica asked.

"What big news? Remember, nobody's talked to me in days."

Fern got all sad-looking. "It's all over—"

Whitney interrupted. "I'll tell her! It's my dream that's been smashed to . . . Amber, what's my dream been smashed to?"

"Smithereens," she answered.

Whitney's bottom lip was pushed out. "I've given up any hope whatsoever of tracking down my sister. So what do you think of *that,* party pooper?"

"Yeah, so what do you think of that?" Fern echoed.

"Man-oh-man, my all-time best thievery from a social worker, and for nothing!"

I still didn't understand. So I wasn't going with them. But excuse me, just because *I* wasn't going didn't mean that *they* couldn't go. I make a loud sound of exasperation and said, "Excuse me, but I don't see any chains around your ankles. What's stopping you?"

"Everything!" Whitney said, and I asked, "Like what?" and Whitney answered, "For one, Amber's dream. We can't go without you. For two, the directions."

This was still making no sense. "I'll write everything down. I'll draw a map."

"Man-oh-man, we'll be wandering all over from here to . . . to . . . where will we be wandering to, Amber?"

"Timbuktu," she said in her soft way.

I opened my mouth to say, *City buses don't run to Timbuktu,* but Whitney was holding up her hand like a traffic cop. "Stripped of my lifelong dream!"

"Gone!" Fern said. "Like that!" She tried to snap her fingers but no sound came out.

∾

When people are being totally illogical, a logical person must step right up and take the situation in hand. All I had to do was get Whitney's sister's address, and, once I wrote out the directions, they would see it didn't take a bus genius to get around. They wouldn't need me.

I left them at the park and rushed back to the Pumpkin House, up the stairs, and locked the bedroom door behind me. I slipped my hand under Whitney's mattress where she kept the stolen papers.

Yuck! Double yuck! She kept a lot more under there than papers. But nothing—not half-eaten apples, sunflower-seed shells, and other slimy, sticky things—would stop me. I was up to my elbow, then my forearm, and then I felt them.

Papers! I pulled out the stack. I figured I would have a lot of reading to do. But then on page 2, I read something. Then I reread what I thought I had just read, and then I read it again.

If anyone had seen me just then, I know what they would have seen. You know what a baby looks like when she's startled, when she's overcome with a sensation like she's falling?

That was me, Cal Lavender, who never gets surprised by much, eyes all bugged out, arms outstretched, breathing stilled. My whole body went rigid, like the whole world had dropped away and nothing solid was left beneath me.

CHAPTER 34

I couldn't wait until they came back, so I rushed to the park. They were lined up on the swings. Perfect!

"I changed my mind. Count me in. Let's go tomorrow. Why wait?"

Whitney dragged her feet to stop swinging. "Um, er, why so soon?"

"Why not? Why keep your sister waiting any longer?"

Monica and Fern did the cheerleading for me: "Yeah, Whitney"—*giggle, giggle*—"why wait? . . . Let's do it! . . . Tomorrow. . . . For sure!"

I said, "You don't look very happy about it, Whitney."

She kept looking at me, trying to know what I knew, trying to know if I knew what she was thinking I might know but couldn't believe I knew.

"Whitney?" Monica asked. "You *are* happy, aren't you?"

"Happy? Of course, I'm happy. Why wouldn't I be happy? Man-oh-man, happy, happy, happy."

Cal Lavender isn't normally a revengeful type of person. But in this case, revenge was going to be very sweet.

∽

Here's what I had read in Whitney's stolen file:

An eighteen-month-old girl was taken into protective custody by the county Department of Children's Services. Whitney S. is the only child of . . . I stopped there. Not wanting to jump to conclusions, I scanned the rest of the file, every word of it.

Here's what I most definitely did not read: Any mention of a sister—past, present, and certainly not future.

CHAPTER 35

Here's how I imagined things would go that night:

ME: It's time to go, Whitney. Tell me your sister's address.

WHITNEY: I can't. *(Whitney falling to the floor in a heap of guilt and remorse)* I can't because I lied! I lied, I tell you. I lied!

A CHORUS OF EVERYONE ELSE: You lied? How could you! Apologize to Cal.

WHITNEY *(at my feet)*: Cal, can you ever forgive me?

ME *(taking my time)*: I'll think about it.

ے

Here's how things actually went that night:

ME: It's time to go, Whitney. Tell me your sister's address.

WHITNEY: Okay.

ME: Okay?

WHITNEY: Okay, but not here. Outside. Man-oh-man, let's get out of here already.

ME: But . . .

WHITNEY *(throwing herself on her stomach and crawling to the bedroom door as though she's an army man, checking to make sure the coast is clear)*: Let's go.

ME: But . . .

WHITNEY *(picking up Ike Eisenhower the Fifth and leading Monica and Fern down the stairs. Voice in a loud whisper)*: Cal! Let's go, Amber!

ME: But . . .

In any life story about Cal Lavender, it would definitely say that she is not the kind of person who gets roped into doing something she doesn't want to do. So why did I follow her down the stairs? I suppose I just wanted to see what Whitney was planning to do. What would she say when she couldn't produce this famous sister?

"Whitney, do we need one token or a pass?" We were standing at the bus stop, waiting for the number 26 to start our journey. I saw her mind scrambling before she answered.

"One token? You gotta be kidding, right? You think it's only one bus ride?"

"A pass then. It's good for all night."

Monica looked worried. "All night? You don't mean like *all* night, do you? I'll get too tired."

For weeks, everyone had been stashing away part of

their allowance, which they now turned over to me. I could tell that the driver of the number 26 wasn't thrilled when I gave him the clinking pile of pennies, nickels, dimes, and quarters. The look he gave me wasn't friendly at all. I assured him that it was the exact amount, but did he believe me? No. Not even when I told him that I was extremely good at math. He had to count every coin himself before handing over our passes.

The number 26 was a long, stop-and-go ride with people getting off and people getting on, and finally, we were there. Downtown. My home turf! Here's where time gets weird again. It seemed like I had been gone for years, yet at the same time it was all so familiar, like I hadn't been gone at all. There was the Thrifty Cuts beauty parlor, and the "Nothing More than 99 Cents" Discount Mart.

I led the way into the bus station and picked up a bus schedule. "So where to?"

"North," Whitney said with so much confidence that I thought for a minute that maybe I was wrong, maybe I had missed something in the file, maybe, in fact, there was a sister and we were on our way there right now. "We want the number 46B bus," I said. "That goes north."

We found the bus waiting and hopped on right before it pulled away from the station. And when we were as far north as we could go, I asked, "Where next?" and Whitney said, "West, all the way," so I checked the schedule and decided we should take the number 17.

By this time, it was getting pretty late and buses were running slow. We stood on a corner for twenty-five minutes waiting for the number 17 to show up. It was empty except for a couple of old, sad-looking guys. I kept waiting for the bus driver to ask what a bunch of ten- and eleven-year-old girls were doing on the number 17 bus at ten o'clock at night, but he never did.

"Can we go south from here?" Whitney asked me.

"If you'd just tell me where we need to go, I could—"

She ignored me and tapped the bus driver on the shoulder. "South?"

"Number 74, ladies," he answered. "Next stop, runs on the hour."

So we got off and we waited and we waited and when the number 74 finally pulled up, we got on, and Whitney handed me Ike Eisenhower the Fifth before grabbing the bus map from me. She ran her index finger from left to right.

"Whitney?" Monica asked.

"Shhhhh. I'm concentrating."

"Whitney?" Monica's skin was kind of green. "I'm getting bus sick. Are we almost there yet?"

Whitney didn't take her nose out of the schedule. "Jeez-Louise, if we were almost there, I would have done this alone months ago. I told you it was far."

So that's how it went. After the 74, we took the 37, the 68A, the 24, the 18, the 6 express (only the express part wasn't running at that time of the night, so there were about a million stops). At some point, everyone stopped talking to everyone else. Even Fern stopped giggling. We just stared out the windows like we were in some kind of public-transportation trance. We went north, east, south, southeast, and northwest until nobody had any idea of where we were.

Even I, the bus genius, was dazed, but I was certain of one thing. We had passed by the same places more than once. Definitely. I was sure of it. But did I bring that up? No!

I also didn't point out that we had taken the 43 north and then twenty minutes later hopped on the 43 south. I didn't say anything because by then I figured out what Whitney was up to. If she kept us moving, maybe we wouldn't figure out that she had no place to go. I said nothing because I knew that all I had to do was wait.

At the corner of Trescony and Langdon Streets, her time finally ran out.

"That's it," Monica announced, holding her stomach. "I'm not getting on another bus."

"Me either," Fern said.

We were in a neighborhood that looked vaguely familiar, but I guess most neighborhoods look like this one did. Houses all lined up with perfect squares of green lawn. Most of the windows were dark. Standing under a street lamp, I squinted at the schedule. "There aren't any more buses until morning."

That did it. Monica and Fern started whining like sick cows. They were starving! They were tired! They should have known better than to trust Whitney! "Cal, do something!" they pleaded.

"Do what?" I said, all innocence. "I could do something if Whitney would tell me the exact address. But Whitney won't do that, will you, Whitney?"

Monica turned on her—"Tell her!"—and Whitney looked so pathetic that I almost felt sorry for her. Only I didn't. I kept pushing. "Why won't Whitney tell me where her sister lives? Why, Whitney?"

"Because . . . ," Whitney was stammering. "Because . . ."

Then Amber, who had been her usual silent self all night, spoke up. "Because we're here. Right, Whitney?"

"Here?" I blurted out. "How do you know?"

Amber's voice was strong, her eyes steady on mine. "Because I dreamed it."

That gave Whitney enough time to wipe the thoroughly confused look off her face. "That's right. Man-oh-man, and you were ready to bail out on me, but here we are. I knew we'd make it, man-oh-man. We did it and now I'm here."

Monica suddenly looked much better. She started

doing this little jumping-up-and-down dance. Fern was clapping her hands and saying, "What now? What now?"

I noticed Whitney turned pleading eyes on Amber for help, but Amber's face remained blank.

I asked pointedly, "So which house? Where does this famous sister live?"

Whitney pointed to a house that looked like every other house, except for a small glow of light coming from a window by the side.

"Let's go!" Now Fern was also jumping up and down.

"No," Amber said. "She's got to go alone."

Whitney looked surprised. "I do? Right. I do." She took a few tentative steps, turned, lifted her hand to wave at us and give us a smile. It was a strange smile, which I suppose is the only smile she could have, considering that she was sneaking up to the house of total strangers and would eventually have to come back and confess the truth to us once and for all.

The way the streetlight was angled gave us a perfect view of Whitney's every move. She crossed the street, climbed over the picket fence, and pressed her body against the side of the house the way the police do in movies before they kick in the door of someone on the Most Wanted list. She edged closer and closer to the glowing light. Then she got down on hands and knees and crept until she was just under the window.

She peeked in, ducked her head below the sill, peeked in again. She stayed in that awkward, uncomfortable position for a long time.

Then, just when I thought Whitney would never come back and face us with the truth, she took a running start across the lawn and hopped the fence like it was nothing but air.

CHAPTER 36

"You should see it!" Whitney said. "Her room is like a palace."

"What color?" Fern wanted to know.

"Purple and orange! My favorites. There's a dog curled up on the floor and a kitten sleeping right on her pillow and a bird, one of those big expensive birds, a Starlight McDraw."

"Scarlet macaw," Amber said.

"Yeah, one of those, and she's got her own phone and I could see in her closet which is packed to the . . . what's it packed to, Amber?"

"Packed to the gills."

"With all sorts of stuff. The people who adopted her aren't cheapskates. She's got three pairs of skates, the expensive kind. And skis and a wall full of medals for gymnastics, which must mean she's the real bouncy type and takes after me."

"You're the younger sister," Monica pointed out. "So you take after her."

"We take after each other!"

Am I, Cal Lavender, the only one here who sees through this charade?

"And, man-oh-man, this next part you won't believe!"

Fern asked a breathless "What?"

"They came in right while I was looking. I ducked so they couldn't see me."

I couldn't help myself. "Who came in?"

"The parents! They look like movie stars, and they stood real close together."

"Like this?" Monica pulled Fern to her side.

"Closer! And they were holding hands and my sister was sound asleep in her big, fancy, everything-matches bed, like this." Whitney lay down on the bus-stop bench and pretended to be asleep. "They moved closer to my sister's bed."

"Like this?" Holding hands, Monica and Fern approached.

"And when they were standing right over her, the parents looked at each other and smiled. And then, the father reached over. Yeah, that's right, Monica, you're the father. And then, he tucked in my sister even though she was already perfectly tucked in!"

"Wow!" Monica said, and Fern sighed, closing her eyes to picture every detail.

Cal Lavender wasn't sucked in one little bit. I don't know what Whitney had been looking at all that time, but

I knew it wasn't a happy ending. I said, "Now we get to meet her, right? This is what we came for, right?"

I was very gratified to see Whitney's mouth tremble around the corners. I had her now. She was out of excuses. It was time for Cal Lavender to bring the truth to the surface. I faced the others. "I hate to break this to you, but Whitney's sister doesn't—"

Amber broke in, "She doesn't need Whitney anymore."

"That's not what I—"

Amber again, "That's why she wanted Whitney to come, to tell her that."

"The truth is—" I insisted.

"The truth is she wants Whitney to know that she's doing fine."

I whirled on her. "Amber, I can't believe you don't know that—"

"What?" She took me by the shoulders until she was looking directly into my face. "What? What truth do I need to know?"

And that's when I knew. I knew that she knew what I knew. I knew that Amber had known the truth about Whitney's sister for a long time, a very long time. Her eyes were daring me and at the same time, pleading with me. "Cal, what do I need to know?"

"That Whitney . . . that Whitney's sister . . ." My voice petered out.

Amber let go of my shoulders. "I know, Cal. I know that Whitney's sister doesn't need her. And Whitney doesn't really need her sister. Not anymore." She turned to Whitney. "Right, Whitney?"

"Why?" I said. I meant: *Why are you covering up for Whitney?* But Amber answered a different question. "Because Whitney has something else. Because you came all this way to help her. And Fern came. And Monica stopped being afraid and came. Whitney doesn't need a sister anymore because Whitney has us."

Being a stomach person, the truth of this hit me you know where. For once, Cal Lavender really didn't know what to say. So when Amber said, "Let's go home now," I didn't argue.

CHAPTER 37

After all those buses, we were only about a mile from the Pumpkin House. We walked in silence, our feet dragging, the streetlights turning us into long shadows. When we got there, the front door was locked. I had been the last one out, and I would never in a million years forget to leave the front door unlatched. That meant trouble.

For some reason, I didn't care. I don't know what anyone else was thinking, but I bet we were all thinking the same thing: *At least we're in trouble together.*

We decided to wait on the back patio. Morning would be here soon enough.

There was light from the full moon back there. I got a jolt seeing the Knitting Lady just sitting there, not trying to hide or anything, just sitting in a sweater, legs crossed, like it was the middle of a sunny afternoon and we were invited guests who had arrived on time for a party. What would she do now? Scold us? Lecture us? Ask for details and explanations?

"Sit," the Knitting Lady said, and pointed to a place next to her. Amber sat on her right, and then Whitney and the others formed a small circle. I was on her left.

"There's a l-little chill that's just coming up. Funny how it does that when it's close to morning."

She reached behind herself and pulled out a piece of knitting with familiar colors—all my yellows and golds. The needles were gone, and she had given it a smooth, finished edge. She handed one end to me and I held it as the other end was passed along. Each of us kept a section and draped it around our shoulders. The Knitting Lady must have known exactly when it was done because it was the perfect fit to cover all of us.

I glanced up. I imagined someone standing at my window and wondered how our group would appear to a stranger. There was an old lady looking a little older and more tired than usual. A girl whose black eye was gone without a trace. A girl whose once-broken arm was already as round and firm as the rest of her. A girl whose hair was almost fully grown in. A girl with a heart that no longer had a hole in it. There was me, looking like a perfectly ordinary eleven-year-old.

Now this is going to sound totally illogical, and by now it must be clear that Cal Lavender is never totally illogical without good reason. But there were others with us on the patio that night. A stranger at the window wouldn't have seen them, but I felt them.

I felt the presence of every girl who had ever passed through the Pumpkin House. Of Lillian and all those kids on the orphan train. I saw traces of them in Whitney, in Amber, in Monica and Fern. And, yes, in myself. We were all there that night, joined together in a tight, knitted circle.

I knew exactly what would happen next. The Knitting Lady had waited and waited until just the right moment. We needed to be ripe. None of us was surprised when she said, "Let's begin. Let's end. The final chapter.

CHAPTER 38

"L-Lillian wasn't even fifteen years old when she made her first professional stage appearance. She wore her hair piled on her head and dressed in a sparkling gown. Right before she started typing, she would always lift the lorgnette to her eyes and gaze out into the audience. It became one of her trademarks. For the first three months, the great H. W. Mergenthal kept Lovely Lillian with her Delightfully Dexterous Digits as the opening act, which was by far the worst spot to be. It took the audience forever to settle down. But she kept practicing and smiling and typing and swaying and eventually moved to fourth place on the bill, right before a new and very popular act called 'the Regurgitator.'"

I blurted out, "What kind of act is that?"

The Knitting Lady threw back her head and laughed: "So you know what *regurgitate* means!"

"Throw up," I said, and Whitney jumped in with more synonyms. "Puke, barf, upchuck, toss your cookies, lunch."

"That's the idea. This young man would swallow mouthfuls of kerosene and then regurgitate. You knew it was the real thing because he aimed at a flame, and that flame would whoosh up like an angry dragon."

"Whoa! Don't try that at home, kids!" Whitney laughed.

"It was Lillian's favorite act, and, at each show, she would stand in the wings transfixed. But it was more than the act that had caught Lillian's fancy. It was the Regurgitator himself. He was a very good-looking young man, with jet-black hair and a fake mustache, which gave him a foreign, mysterious look that audiences admired. The Regurgitator returned Lillian's attentions. He admired her spunk, her determination, and also the way she looked in those glamorous gowns. These two took one look at each other and sensed that they were two of a kind. They had an immediate understanding, much the way girls in the Pumpkin House have an understanding with one another, even though you don't always like to admit it. You see, the Regurgitator was also an orphan and a runaway, so he knew what it meant to feel alone in the world.

"It's an old story what happened next, and I think you're all mature enough to picture how it happened. It was only natural that these two young people started spending more time together, clinging to each other emotionally and physically during long train rides from town to town. Lillian became pregnant and gave birth to a baby girl. Does anyone remember Lillian's daughter's name?"

When no one answered, the Knitting Lady began

tossing out clues. "An all-night drive. Fruit trees in bloom. Throne? Little Raven?"

Black hair with purple streaks. Orphanage with plum trees. I remembered. "Brenda! The girl from the beginning of the story. The one who was dropped off at the orphanage. She threw the lorgnette on the ground when her mother drove away."

Whitney couldn't believe it. "Man-oh-man, *that* mother! That was Lillian?"

"It w-was."

"Even I remember!" Fern said. "I don't like that mother."

"Me either," Monica said. "She just dumped off her kid."

The Knitting Lady directed the next question to me: "I recall that you didn't much like her either at the beginning of the story. But now? What do you think of Lillian now?"

I didn't know *what* to think. "I don't like what she did to Brenda. I really don't like it! But at the same time, I can't *not* like Lillian. All the things that happened to her? All the things that she went through? I don't like her, but I *do*."

"You understand her now," the Knitting Lady said. "When you understand someone, when you see the path of her life, the choices she had to make, the things that stood in her way, the hurdles she leaped, things get more complicated. It's no longer ... Amber, what is it no l-longer?"

"Cut and dried," she said.

"Black and white," I added.

"Exactly," Whitney said.

Fern was chewing on her knuckle. "I have a question. Did Lillian become a big star?"

The Knitting Lady put it simply: "No."

"Why not?" Monica asked. "She practiced and set the world record. She was the best!"

"S-sometimes, unfortunately, the best is not enough. That's not to say that Lillian ever stopped trying. She dragged her daughter, Brenda, across the country, but she never became the headliner she wanted to be."

"That's not fair," I pointed out.

"Since when is life always fair?"

I had no answer for that. I just listened as the Knitting Lady explained. "The problem was Lillian's timing. By the time Brenda was six, vaudeville was taking its last gasp of breath. Between the movies and radio, people were no longer so impressed by fast typing and fire-spitting. Like a lot of other performers, Lillian decided to go to California and try to make it as a movie star."

Whitney asked, "What happened to ... to who, Amber?"

"The Regurgitator."

"Before B-Brenda was born, he joined another company."

I asked, "So the man who was driving when they dropped Brenda at the orphanage? That wasn't him?"

"Not her father, no." She paused to let that sink in and then told us that we were forgetting to ask the most important question.

"Why?" Whitney asked.

Amber said, "Why didn't she take Brenda to California, too?"

"That's the qu-question, all right."

For once, the Knitting Lady looked as confused as Fern usually looked. She swallowed hard. "This very question plagued Brenda her whole life. She never really stopped trying to find a satisfying answer. I can't believe it was simple selfishness on Lillian's part. No! I have to believe that she thought she was doing what was best for her child."

"But Brenda didn't like it!" I said. "She didn't like it one little bit."

The Knitting Lady asked if I thought Brenda missed all the excitement of her former life, all the moving about and the closeness she had with her mother.

I said, "Yes, ma'am. I know for a fact that she did."

"D-do you think there was anything that Brenda actually liked about living in the Home?"

"No," Monica said quickly.

"M-maybe just one thing?"

"Maybe," I said, "she liked being around kids her own age—but only if the kids weren't mean to her, which I hope they weren't. Were they?"

"K-kids are kids. Sometimes, they can be very hurtful, especially if they've been hurt themselves. But other times, they made Brenda feel very much at home."

"And worrying," Monica said. "I bet Brenda didn't miss worrying about her mother all the time."

"Safe," Amber said. "She liked feeling safe."

"All that!" the Knitting Lady said. "So that's it. The end of the story."

The end? I wasn't the only one who thought she heard wrong.

"The end?" Fern repeated. "Did I miss something?"

I thought: *This can't possibly be the end.*

So I said, "It would be a totally unfair thing to leave us hanging like that, especially after what we've been through tonight."

Whitney's head snapped from me to the Knitting Lady. "Don't ask what we've been through tonight. Just tell the end of the story."

"That's it. I'm d-done."

We all protested—"You're not!"—which made the Knitting Lady mutter that this was her story and she should certainly know when she was done telling it.

Monica said, "No story ends like that."

And then Whitney went, "It's not just your story any-more. It's our story now, and we know it's not finished."

"Your story?" the Knitting Lady asked. "Is it, now? Is it your story? If it's your story, then you should be able to finish it yourselves."

I didn't understand. "You mean make up the ending?"

The Knitting Lady held up a finger, the same finger she used to poke through the mistakes in my knitting. "You're all quite capable of completing the story because you have all the information you need to work it out. So wh-wh-wh-wh . . ."

She stopped, took a breath. "So what becomes of Brenda?"

"Did she ever get adopted?" Whitney asked.

"N-no."

"Did she ever see her mother again?"

"No. But she n-never forgot her."

"Did Brenda ever have kids?"

"At some p-point in her life, Brenda made up her mind that she would never be like other people. She went numb inside. She closed up like a—"

"Stop it," Amber said. "I don't like this part of the story. I don't want to hear any more."

The Knitting Lady pulled her closer, gathering her into a hug. "It doesn't mean that Brenda didn't have a family, only that hers was a different kind of family. Her whole adult life, Brenda surrounded herself with kids."

Now Amber's voice came in soft, eager—"She did?"—
and Fern asked, "What kind of kids?"

"K-kids who like to hear stories."

"Like us?" Monica asked.

"Exactly l-like you."

I asked, "Why did she tell stories?"

"B-because the kids needed to hear them and Brenda
needed to tell them. It was like she was chosen by something larger than herself. Oh, she had her doubts. She
often wondered why someone so shy, someone who was
always tripping and stumbling over her words, had somehow been picked to tell the stories."

"Tripping and stumbling?" I asked.

"Oh, d-didn't I mention that before? As a young girl,
her stutter was quite pronounced and it embarrassed her.
But at some point in her life, she stopped asking why she
felt compelled to tell stories and just told them."

We all went quiet then. The first light of morning was
coming into the backyard. It was spectacular, like sunrise
over the Grand Canyon or some other place that a city girl
such as myself had never seen in person, but that was the
way I imagined it would be. Maybe there was something
special in the air that morning to create such a sunrise. Or
maybe it was a reflection of the light—*snap!*—that was
going on inside each of us.

I asked, "This Brenda?"

"Y-yes, Cal?"

"This girl who lived in the Home? Who never saw her mother again? Who grew up and told stories?"

The Knitting Lady stood, stretched her arms over her head. Even with all the wrinkles, I could see what she must have looked like as a kid, her hair long and purple-black, hanging down in two ponytails. And even though everyone, even Fern, knew the answer, I asked the question anyway, just to finish the story in the proper way. "This girl Brenda? Is she you?"

The Knitting Lady gave a big yawn, but I could see teasing behind her eyes as she said:

"Now, girls, whatever gave you that idea?"

CHAPTER 39

Isn't this just the way life is?

For weeks and weeks, I had been waiting for the front door of the Pumpkin House to swing open, for Betty to sweep in and for my real life to begin again. So wouldn't you know it? Just when I had settled in and arrived at the conclusion that this particular life and these particular people were my real life as much as any other, the door *did* swing open. In walked Mrs. S. the social worker, who told me to pack my bags.

"You're going home," she said.

It happened just like that.

At the front door, they lined up to say good-bye. Monica had her arm looped around the shoulder of giggling Fern. "Man-oh-man," Whitney said. "Don't ever forget the girl who kicked heart disease's butt."

"And Ike Eisenhower the Fifth," I said.

I hugged Amber the hardest. She brushed away her new bangs, playfully, like a puppy.

Then the Knitting Lady was standing in front of me, no longer exactly eye to eye. I must have grown half an inch since that first day. When she handed me a set of knitting needles and a brand-new ball of yarn, I tried not to tear up because Cal Lavender is not the type to make a big whoop-de-do fuss about something as ordinary as a ball of pumpkin-colored yarn. But my eyes started burning a little, and it felt like warm little bugs moving down my cheeks. They rolled and rolled.

"Get out the windshield wipers," Whitney said, which embarrassed me at first, until I noticed that I wasn't the only one who needed those wipers.

The social worker drove. I sat in the back. I had a million questions, but I didn't ask them. Instead, I started knitting. I didn't know what I was making. I just trusted that when the yarn ran out I would have the exact pumpkin-colored thing that I needed.

When Betty saw me, she didn't say anything. Which, if you knew Betty, was a full-blown miracle. She cupped her hands on my shoulders and just looked at me in a way that made time and space disappear.

I remembered what the Knitting Lady had warned: Sometimes love isn't enough.

But sometimes it is.

Maybe now is where you're dying to hear about how I went on to live a very typical, average life. But I could never be a typical eleven-year-old—or twelve- or thirteen-year-old, for that matter.

True, Betty learned plenty about what it means to be the grown-up in the family. But Betty was still Betty. When she got the itch, we moved. I didn't always get to bed at a decent time or make it to school, but I still managed to learn more than the average kid.

If I ever do get around to writing my life story, it will say: *Cal Lavender had adventures you can't believe. Just ask her sometime.*

I never again saw Whitney and Amber, Monica and Fern, but I thought about them a lot. In a way, you can say that I never stopped thinking about them. I knew they were out there, thinking about me, too, about the Knitting Lady's story, pulling on the threads of our shared history to create their own life stories.

And I bet one thing. I bet that their stories are like mine in one way—anything but typical and ordinary. After all, that's what kids like us call life.

AUTHOR'S NOTE

The Knitting Lady's Guide to Making a Scarf

One of the best things about knitting is that you don't need much to get started—just two needles and a ball of yarn. Don't forget good lighting and your peace of mind.

I recommend starting with medium-weight yarn. It doesn't have to be expensive, but wool or a wool blend is good—it stretches and won't make your hands all sweaty. Use needles that are at least size 9. The bigger the needle, the faster the knitting goes, but don't get something that's too cumbersome for your hands. Plastic needles are good, but I like wooden needles best—they aren't slick and don't let stitches slide off when you aren't looking.

The first step is *casting on*, which creates the first row of stitches on one of the needles. This can be pretty intimidating for a beginner, so find someone to do this for you. (It's fun and you can learn it later.) Ask the person to cast on between 15 and 20 stitches for a scarf, depending on the width you like.

It's time to knit. Holding the needle with the stitches in your left hand, angle the point to the right. With your right hand, put the tip of the empty needle into the first stitch, from front to back, making an X with the tips.

Hold both needles at the X in your left hand. Using your right hand, loop the yarn from the ball up and away from you. Then bring the yarn toward you and down between the two needles. Whew! Got that? It sounds more complicated than it is.

Now, keeping tension on the wrapped yarn, bring the tip of the right needle (with the wrapped yarn) through the loop on the left needle to the front. Is the right needle now in front of the left one? You got it!

Almost done. Just slide the right needle up and away until the loop on the left needle drops off and you have a new stitch on the right. Congratulations! You just completed your first knit stitch.

Continue knitting until the left needle is empty and you have a row of gorgeous new stitches on the right needle. Switch sides now—move the needle with the stitches to your left hand—and start a new row. Keep going until your scarf is the length you like and ask someone to *bind off* for you. That's another fun thing you can learn once you become a whiz with the basic stitch.

As you knit, don't forget the Knitting Lady's mantra: *In through the front door / run around the back / peek through the window / off jumps Jack.*

If you want more ideas about knitting, like how to make a scarf with lots of colorful stripes and a fringe, check out my Web site: www.jillwolfson.com.